SECRET BILLIONAIRE

Jess Gilmour is upended by her new holiday let guest, Gabe Garrett. This Texan cowboy is not the irascible and stubborn rancher he's been billed as — and the more Jess gets to know Gabe, the more she's intrigued . . . Gabe doesn't support his brother's move to Scotland, but from the moment he arrives in Jess's lochside corner of the highlands, Gabe realises he's the one who must change. But Gabe is a cowboy with a secret of his own . . .

Books by Judy Jarvie
in the Linford Romance Library:

PITCHED INTO LOVE

mm 308

JUDY JARVIE

SECRET BILLIONAIRE

Complete and Unabridged

LINFORD
Leicester

First published in Great Britain in 2012

First Linford Edition
published 2013

*A catalogue record for this book is available
from the British Library.*

ISBN 978–1–4448–1719–5

Published by
F. A. Thorpe (Publishing)
Anstey, Leicestershire

Set by Words & Graphics Ltd.
Anstey, Leicestershire
Printed and bound in Great Britain by
T. J. International Ltd., Padstow, Cornwall

This book is printed on acid-free paper

1

Gabe Garrett had the air of a mustang with a grudge. Sporting dust smears, dark stubble and the dent of his discarded Stetson, Gabe stood to full height in his favourite work boots with palms on hips. Gun-slinger without a weapon.

He cast a long shadow across The Lucky Star Saloon's backroom floor as he glared at his sister's back view. 'You didn't listen, did you?'

'Ah. You got the package,' his sister, Nancy said on a half-sigh as she turned and her smile disappeared. 'The tickets and booking documents. And instead of taking it on the chin you're here ready for war with me.'

Nancy was midway through mixing a pitcher of some lurid red-coloured cocktail. It matched her varnished nails. The scarlet hue reminded him he was here for final warnings and a stop sign. He dreaded to think what was in the drink mix.

Not only had Nancy ignored their earlier discussions, she'd now forced Gabe into a tight conscience corner. He didn't intend to comply.

'I wondered how long it would take for you to seize the offensive,' Nancy added in a tone that made his blood pressure hike up. Gabe shot her an accusing look; the stern one that made novice ranch-hands quake.

'I'm not going — plain, simple. And final.'

Nancy's eyebrows rose and stayed high. She stared him out but Gabe could tell by the tapping toe that the bravado was faked. She twiddled the cowboy boot again.

'Why are you so stubborn?' Nancy accused.

'Interrogation and guilt trips won't change my mind, sis.'

Nancy flicked her chestnut curls. 'Somebody has to kick sense into your knuckle-bone head. It's our brother's wedding. You can't not go; I won't let you.'

Gabe bit back the urge to turn around and leave. Why did Nancy take Josh's side? He was halfway tempted to yank her out to the ranch and shut her in the big black barn.

'I have a ranch to run. He has a life of his own now.'

The wedding had been a burr under his peace of mind for months. The last thing Gabe needed was pressure. And what he really didn't want was to fly to a foreign country to eat humble pie and play best man at a wedding he didn't want to be at. Even if it was his brother Josh's.

Nancy raised her eyes. 'See, hurt pride. Big ol' Gabe has to be the one callin' the shots.' Nancy stirred the pitcher so hard the liquid sloshed near the rim. 'Can't you just be happy and accept for Momma's sake?'

Gabe resisted the urge to discard the pitcher down the drain — or drink it in one to show how she'd riled him. Gabe didn't drink, but Nancy was pushing him close now.

He palmed dusty, dark tufts of his hair. 'To heck with weddings in Scotland — it's of no concern to me.'

Gabe knew he lied. His brother marrying and choosing Scotland over Texas brought heaps of concern. How could the Garrett dynasty have come to this?

But Josh's mind was made up, end of story.

'You have a team who'll handle the ranch. They're big boys and it's Broken Bridle Ranch, not a royal dynasty,' said Nancy. 'Stop making problems; get off your high horse.'

'It's Scotland, Nancy.'

'Scotland, Europe. Not the moon.' Her free hand slid onto her hip. 'Where's your adventurous spirit, cowboy?'

Gabe took the cocktail mixer stick from Nancy's fingers. 'You just wasted your hard-earned dollars on an air ticket because I'm still not going.' He could feel his tightened chest as he spoke the words.

'I'm not taking no for an answer,' Nancy retorted with force that surprised him. There was anger, pure and fiery in long lashed, green eyes. 'Or it won't just be a brother you've lost. You'll lose a sister too.'

Gabe realised he'd underestimated how deep this went for Nancy. Wake up call to self. For some moments Gabe couldn't find the right words to reply with.

He shook his head and whispered. 'Emotional blackmail as a bonus extra?'

'If you don't go — then I guess I'll lose the respect I have for you. It's getting more dented every time we argue.'

With her dainty chin thrust out, Nancy reminded him that she was never one to hide from conflict.

Gabe muttered like a curse. 'He walked out. Figured he was owed his dream. Figured we'd work out what to do without him. He had no care for

Broken Bridle when he left us all behind. He's gone and now we have to go celebrate?'

'He followed his heart and fell in love. You'd deny your brother happiness?'

A red blush stained Nancy's cheeks before her eyes brimmed with tears. Something hit sharply inside his gut.

'Momma would make you see you're wrong.'

'Momma isn't here, sis. And if she was, Josh wouldn't have gone away.'

Nancy blotted her tears with a tissue and with a long, low sigh Gabe drew out the stool from the counter and sat.

'He won't appreciate me bein' there. We haven't spoken in over a year.'

Nancy's gaze speared him. 'All the more reason to try.' She took his hands in hers. He could smell her fruity perfume; as fresh and bursting with sweet energy as she was. Gabe was proud of her, even if she did drive him to crazy town and back on a bronco. She slid one hand around his shoulders.

His little sister still regarded him as a hero and clung to him like a rock.

Nancy put her face on his shoulder. 'I want my brothers talkin' again.'

Gabe had that sinking feeling. He closed his eyes. 'Of all the places — Scotland. Mountains and castles . . . '

'Fairytale lochs and history and romance.'

Gabe aped a grimace then pushed back the stool which screeched across the floor tiles. He was weary. He'd come on a mission and failed.

'I'll think about it. That's as good as it's gettin'.'

'I'm on your side. Always will be, Gabriel Garrett.'

Gabe rubbed his neck, feeling cornered and confused. 'Funny way of showin' that.'

'I love you, brother, but if you stay in Tall Trees Creek, Texas while your brother gets married to the love of his life in a castle in Scotland . . . well, you'll be the one with regrets.'

Nancy added fruit to her mixture

then picked up her pitcher. 'We done here?'

'You seem to be.'

She nodded and left him watching the door.

Full points to the woman serving drinks.

* * *

Re-arranging stock in Pure Pleasures had lately become a task best achieved by an acrobat. Or someone with proficiency on stilts.

Sadly Jess Gilmour only realised this as she teetered on her seen-better-days step ladder and over-stretched to stow a basket on its shelf.

The ladder swayed, her foot jerked and she grabbed out. When her flailing fingers found the wall, Jess balanced gingerly, afraid to move. Or breathe.

Her friend Ruth had warned her earlier.

'Don't overstretch yourself, Jess. You're running yourself into the ground.'

She'd been talking about work

obligations — from The Crofter's Flask Inn to her pride and joy soap shop business, Pure Pleasures. Invergarry may be a rural highland backwater in Scotland, but for Jess it was a busy place to be.

Disaster struck as the basket slipped, decanting lavender heads in a fast speed shower and falling with a thud on the floor. The ladder shook and Jess felt panic rise as she wedged a toe against the counter.

'Help!' she muttered; a fruitless plea because she was all alone in the shop, about to fall from a ladder. As if by magic, the door bells jangled to herald a visitor's arrival as Jess let out a strangled yelp, 'I'm in trouble.'

Loud footsteps approached and firm, unseen hands gripped her from behind. The ladder fell with a clatter as she was lifted clear. A sharp male sigh accompanied the movement and Jess was swiftly steadied then lifted with easy strength, then lowered as woody male cologne spiced the air, awakening her senses.

'You like climbing walls?' The voice was deep and caramel rich; its owner's identity, still a complete mystery.

But right now Jess was trying to get her breath back after near disaster, while the nearness of the stranger made the tiny hairs on her arms stand to attention.

'Sorry . . . I got too adventurous there,' Jess muttered as confusion mixed a Molotov cocktail for her nerves. 'I mean, sorry to commandeer you into helping me.'

'You're going to have to mend your ways in future,' the voice added darkly. 'Dangerous tricks like that aren't sensible.'

Jess didn't recognise his deep American tones; he must be a tourist. And fortunately, he'd just saved her from calamity with hands that still gripped her shoulders firmly.

She regained her balance then tucked her hair behind her ears. Then Jess turned when he let her go. She already felt like a foolhardy kid caught climbing an apple tree in roller skates. But when she glanced at her rescuer, she needed a fresh breath of air. Like the near-miss fall, he was breathtaking. As in gorgeous.

And equally hazardous.

Tall, rugged, dark brown hair, green eyes and smoothly worn denims the colour of a summer sky.

The grin and dimples could stop traffic. The build of a gladiator made her feel dwarfed beside him. She definitely hadn't expected a man mountain with a profile worthy of sculpture to appear in her store.

'You timed your entrance very well. Thank you.' She knew she was blushing hard.

The cowboy raised a brow and his eyes glittered as his gaze pierced hers. 'Maybe playing Spiderwoman solo isn't a great move? Next time wear a safety-hat.'

Jess hoped the internal heat inside her would subside. 'I don't think there will be a next time. I'll wait until I have back-up. Or a better ladder.'

Jess drew in a steadying breath as the crazy palpitations and her hormones settled. It wasn't every day she was picked up by a movie hero look-alike. Jess worked hard to conceal her thrumming jitters.

Green eyes stared hard into hers and it was only then she realised that he'd discarded a Stetson cowboy hat on the floor when he'd run to catch her. Breaking her gaze from the hat — and the view of tight jeans as he bent to collect it — she noticed that his lips were full and broad and his hair was sun mottled. He walked back to the counter twirling the hat in long fingers.

'So you're OK?'

'Will be once my heartbeat calms.'

Understatement. And it's the man that's causing the heart-tempo.

'We all get caught out sometimes.' The cowboy gave her a roguish smile. 'If you ever drop by my ranch you'll probably find me dusty and indisposed. Hazard of the job.' His accent was as tempting as honeycomb; women back home must drool.

The women in Invergarry would be queuing for an eyeful of this handsome cowboy. She wondered where he was staying and if he had plans to stay long.

'Doubt if I'd catch you if you fell,' Jess added, forcing a smile.

'Guess it would be fun to try,' he answered and multiplied her blush-quota to maximum.

Jess gulped. There was something about this man that made her senses sprint wildly. Not just the looks but the voice, the designer dimple, the attitude.

Dressed in denim — jacket and jeans — with his sunglasses tucked into his jacket pocket, he filled the space in a manner that didn't happen every day. Usually Jess considered herself lucky if a customer wasn't a neighbouring stray sheep, stopping by to nibble her jute rugs.

He narrowed his eyes to assess her shelving arrangements and looked around Pure Pleasures, her fragrant, traditional, hand-made skincare and soap store. It was a feminine world of skin balms and body preparations. Her extensive ranges of paper-wrapped soap bars were piled high and flanked by pampering potions in gleaming bottles.

'Interesting store,' he remarked.

'Interesting meaning strong smelling. And possibly too girly?' she ventured, filling in the gaps in his comment.

She watched as he toured the store with long, slow strides and boots that punctuated every step.

He glanced at her and remarked back, 'I've worked with cattle that smelled so bad they probably injured my senses for life. I figure this smells pretty good — but my sister would appreciate all this more than me.'

'Feel free to browse. Your sister may like a gift-box keepsake? There are gift baskets too. Shout if you need advice.'

He watched her and softly said, 'I'm no expert but you might wanna fix your hair, ma'am?'

Jess realised she was still wearing spilled lavender heads and it probably lent her the look of a wild, crazy scarecrow. Bad hair day just to round off the ritual humiliation.

She blushed then flicked the debris away, then picked up a bottle from a shelf. 'Have some Wild Heather and Ginger Bath Soak. A thank you gift for saving me. On the house. Maybe your sister will like it — it's unisex too.'

Her cowboy saviour took it from her fingers, first studying the bottle carefully then looking genuinely surprised.

'No thanks required. Just doin' my neighbourly good deed. I'm looking to book in to my accommodation here; at Rowan Croft. I'm here to stay for a while.'

Jess tried to cover her surprise. 'You're in the right place, Sir. You've a booking here?'

The cowboy nodded. 'Three week cottage let.' The cowboy simply watched her levelly and held out a large broad hand for her to shake. 'I'm Josh Garrett's brother Gabe. My flights were delayed so I'm later than planned.'

Jess wiped her dusty hands down her linen apron and shook his hand. 'I'm Jess. Jess Gilmour. I own the shop and run the holiday cottages too.'

Josh was marrying her best friend Ruth in two weeks' time and his brother was a much-anticipated guest. This was the guy who'd caused Ruth sleepless nights and somehow his eye-candy appeal waned for that knowledge.

'You're Josh's brother; the best man. From Texas,' she clarified. 'I was told you wouldn't be arriving until much later.'

'Direct from Broken Bridle Ranch, Tall Trees Creek.'

Jess felt her interest in the man falter. He'd been the fly in the ointment of Ruth's bridal joy. He'd refused to come and yet somehow backed down at the last minute. A cowboy full of contradictions.

16

And he'd been booked to stay at Rowan Croft, her holiday let cottage, by his sister; further underlining his oppositional attitude.

He held his hat over his chest. 'First time in Scotland. First vacation in nearly a decade, too.'

Jess nodded, then jumped to more practical enquiries. 'I thought your connections were cancelled. Thought you were stranded due to flight problems?'

Gabe shrugged. 'I rearranged connections but I didn't think to call ahead to warn you. Pardon me for the oversight, ma'am.'

It would have been nice to know but she kept that to herself. She also considered he was lucky she'd had a late cancellation to permit his sister to make his booking in the first place.

Gabriel Garrett was touted as a surly ranch owner who held his views firm. Stern, irascible, a workaholic loner who preferred horses to people.

He must be difficult when he

wouldn't even stay in his brother's Scottish home.

As if affirming her suspicions Gabe stated, 'The guy next to me on the airplane was full of complaints about the delays. He missed meetings and was talking about his intention to sue for damages.'

Jess's opinionated streak kicked in swiftly. 'Surely flight safety is the highest priority?'

Gabe stared at her. 'I guess some people can't ditch pressing responsibilities.'

Jess's impressions were underlined. Clearly he held all his grudges tight.

Gabe added. 'The sat nav's kaput on my hire car. And given the B-roads and lack of signage, I'm lucky I got here at all.'

Jess resisted the urge to undermine his assertions but the itch to parry back kicked hard. 'D'you rely on sat navs back home on the range?'

Gabe stood erect and eyed her warily. 'Worked Broken Bridle since I was outta diapers. I don't need navigation aids. Know my territory in a blindfold.'

Jess concluded his anti-Scotland feelings were still on max setting, while her sympathy was fixed firm on low.

Jess removed her apron, then took the cottage keys from their hook on the wall, donning a brisk smile as she did so. 'I hope you won't find Rowan Croft too limiting, Mr Garrett. The bed is king-sized. We have hot and cold running water. It's not home, but it's habitable.'

Gabriel Garrett walked close, so tall and dark that he caused a stark shadow to fall across her counter and block out the daylight. 'Glad to be here. I'd rather avoid the wedding fever chaos and the family inquisitions at my brother's place.'

Jess pushed on in an affable tone. 'But surely weddings are a happy family time? Not every day your brother gets married.'

Gabe pocketed his bath soak bottle then replaced his Stetson firmly. 'Guess some folks like fuss more than others.'

Jess cleared her throat. 'Ready for a tour?'

'I guess I am. I'd kinda like to freshen up as it happens.'

As Gabe Garrett retrieved his bags Jess tried to regain equilibrium as images of how that big, worked-out cowboy's body would struggle to squeeze into her cottage's tiny tub. It was a body that sent hot lust spiralling through every nerve ending inside her.

Jess reminded herself that Gabe Garrett was not a man she should ever risk admiring.

For one, he was opposed to the wedding; for two, he didn't want to be here at all. Would he surely complain about the cottage's deficiencies later?

Too bad. He'd just have to live with it. She wasn't making special concessions.

Gabe nodded to her rickety ladder. 'You should dispose of that hazard, ma'am. I'd be happy to do the honours.'

Jess faked her brightest smile and opened the shop door for him. 'You're a guest here, Mr Garrett. Leave store management to me since you're officially here on vacation.'

2

'I'm sorry, Jess, but the chef's off sick and Maura's away. We need urgent help in the kitchen right now.'

Jess's heart plummeted as she listened to the pleading edge in Heather's voice. Her head waitress didn't push it and was an asset to the pub; Jess didn't want to lose her. But at 6pm after a full working day her body wanted to scream at the prospect of a looming pub kitchen shift.

'If there was anyone else, we'd ask them.'

'I'm leaving right now so don't worry. See you shortly.' Jess replaced the handset and tucked her disappointment deep as she untied her apron and stowed it on its hook then grabbed her handbag.

The problem with owning three thriving businesses in a small Highland village was that when the cavalry was needed, you were usually the only option for miles. Tonight was like that and it didn't matter that she already felt dead on her feet.

She'd been making soap batches all day, staffing the store during a coach trip rush too. Her feet ached but since other options were sparse, she headed out to her van to go to The Crofter's Flask just as Gabe Garrett stooped beneath the wisteria entwined arch over Rowan Croft's twisting garden path.

Timing was lousy tonight on all counts.

Jess felt her breath quicken and push inside her for release. She feigned a relaxed smile and wished her composure would hold out better when it came to her new guest.

He looked great too. Way too good for a man who'd endured such a long journey and should be feeling jet lagged. Too good for a man who'd been a bugbear for his brother's bride.

'Ma'am, beautiful evening,' Gabe

called over in greeting. He looked pensive — and his profile was well and truly wasted on ranching. A runway for male models would be far more fitting.

From a distance his legs were so long she wondered how he'd gotten under the arch in the first place.

He'd ditched the western hat now and changed clothes; an open necked sky blue shirt and smart navy jeans replaced his prior travel denims. The added touch of blossom petals from the trellis brushing his dark head caused a frisson of awareness — and perhaps panic — to lodge behind Jess's breastbone. She schooled herself to calm down and relax because, reason number one, she shouldn't be finding Gabriel Garrett attractive. Nor should she be staring. Or losing her cool.

'Settled in? Room OK for you?' Jess asked tentatively.

His gaze made something spark inside her. He didn't smile, simply nodded. 'It's a very clean, neat cottage. Cosy I think you Brits call it. Homely we'd call it back home.'

'Too small?' Jess suggested way too fast.

'And why would I think that?' He flicked her an accusing look.

Jess shrugged awkwardly. 'I just figured it might not be your kind of place.'

Gabe cut in, seeing her discomfort. 'Look, I may have reservations about being here but now that I am I'm going to be happy at your cottage — it's much better than I expected. Ten out of ten.'

Gabe stared at her hard, chastising with his hooded gaze. 'You must learn not to pre-empt negatives, Ms Gilmour. Your cottage is exactly what I need. I live on a ranch, not in a palace. And this is isolated and peaceful — I like it.'

'Oh. Good.' Jess gulped to try and shift the whirling thoughts that were spinning her out of whack.

It wasn't like her to be so phased by a guy. Or so unsure of a business she prided herself on. *Get a grip,* she implored. She forced a wide smile and swiftly changed topic. 'Going out for an evening stroll?'

'Dinner. My brother's summoned me to meet his fiancée at the local inn. Maybe tomorrow I'll get some time to explore.'

Unsure of whether a dinner between Josh, Ruth and Gabe would be a good thing or an imminent combustible conflict, Jess shrugged.

'So you're heading to The Crofter's?'

She watched him intently but his expression gave nothing away. She hoped the fact that Gabe was here in Invergarry surely meant he was attempting a truce with his brother?

'I am.'

'I can offer you a ride if you like.'

Gabe seemed to weigh up her offer. 'Wouldn't be an inconvenience?'

'Not at all. I'm glad you're getting together. Ruth's lovely — a dear friend of mine. She's beautiful, inside and out.' She motioned to the loch. 'And this little loch beside us is Loch Garry;

a rare birds breeding area though not as big as Loch Dinnoch beside the pub. It's vast and you can take a boat trip right across it to the ancient monastery on the island there. Just be careful of the midges when you're loch spotting — tiny insects with a merciless bite that can wreck any holiday. I make a skin balm — remind me to give you some.' She smiled awkwardly because again he was staring so hard it made her uneasy.

There was a long pause before Gabe commented, 'Magic potions are your specialty, Ms Gilmour?'

'Natural cures and remedies, Mr Garrett. Not hubble bubble or devil worship. You don't see any value in herbal cures and the power of nature's gifts?'

He drew closer and she was as aware of his very male chiselled jaw as she was of his impressive height and strong, broad shoulders.

Gabe stared right at her and said

softly, 'I know you don't like me. Won't sharing a ride be fraternising with the enemy?'

Jess swivelled to watch him. 'Why would you think that?' She attempted to regain dignity and courage in her dealings with the cowboy who'd clearly detected her frosty feelings.

'Call it a cowboy's instincts. And I'm guessing as Ruth's friend you figure I've been outta line.'

'You're my guest, and as such you deserve all the help I can offer. Whatever situation has occurred between you and your brother has no bearing on our professional relationship.'

She could see from the twitch of his full lips that he was itching to laugh at her.

'Then let's call a truce. I've come to Scotland and I'm trying hard to build bridges. Call me Gabe. Since I'm the best man and you're maid of honour, I figure less formal works best.'

'Whatever leads to better relations.' Jess tucked her hands in her pockets then remembered that she really should be getting down the road to help at the pub.

Jess opened the van door wide. 'We'd better be going. I own The Crofter's; I have to help there tonight.'

Gabe moved closer and immediately filled the space beside her with his strong, rugged proportions. Something inside Jess's ribcage did percussion very loudly in her ears. He was all man — and she was more intensely aware of him than she'd ever been before of any stranger.

Bad idea. All round.

After all, he disliked the idea of his brother marrying the most wonderful woman he could ever hope to meet.

OK, so Gabe did have some things going for him — she'd be lying to deny it. He was tall and confident. His intense gaze was disconcerting. His obvious stern approach combined with a lack of ease made him all the more heart-stoppingly arresting. And confusing. Like an unpredictable encounter she wasn't quite able to translate. And that penetrating green gaze made something inside her heart react.

But he was still bad. He made her nervous and unsure of herself. And she hated that above all else.

You don't do men. Even handsome ones, she reminded herself sternly.

Wasn't Dan a learning curve to ensure steering clear of difficult men?

Jess checked her watch hastily. 'Sorry to rush you but I'm pushed for time.' Jess climbed into the driver's side.

'I'm grateful for the ride,' he answered. 'All this driving on the other side of the road is still at 'getting the hang of it' stage. Plus I'm far more comfortable on a horse than behind a wheel.'

'Your future sister-in-law owns the stables here. A horse could be organised.'

Gabe frowned. 'I can stay saddle-free for two weeks.'

'Not what I heard.'

Gabe replied softly. 'Ah, you really

have been listening to gossip about the big, bad brother. The one who needs to get a life and stop spoiling everybody's fun.'

Jess corrected, reversing the van. 'Actually, Josh's words were — 'my brother was born on a horse. He'll probably die on one too. But he's coming to my wedding and I want him beside me when I say my vows.''

Gabe stared hard as silence spanned. His green eyes were like sharp agates on hers. Then he fixed his attention straight ahead through the window.

'At one time I figured losing my brother would kill me. Dying on a horse ain't the worst that could happen.'

A tint of blush crept over his cheekbones as he issued the stark confidence.

Jess intook a breath then softly said, 'You're not losing him, Gabe. In fact you're getting a lovely sister-in-law. Josh loves Ruth. And they say love conquers all.'

His voice was smoky when he

answered. 'Ever lost someone; someone you never, ever imagined would bail out on you?'

Jess stared right back, unflinching.

If only he knew her truths.

She'd lost the husband. The self-respect. The dreams. And the grip on who she was. These days she relied on nobody but herself. She had way more experience than Gabe even realised.

The topic had veered uncomfortably close to personal experience. She knew exactly how it felt to suddenly become alone.

'He's not bailing out and you're here now supporting him. Focus on the positives.'

'Easier said than done.' Gabe Garrett didn't meet her gaze but stared ahead.

Jess breathed deeply. She sensed Gabe still really resented being here at all. Was he really here to support his brother — or here to try and take him back home again? To win the war?

The best she could do was step away

from the feud and ignore Gabe Garrett as much as possible.

★　★　★

Jess knew she must decide what to do with The Crofter's Flask — preferably before she keeled over from exhaustion.

Pure Pleasures was her passion; the pub her inheritance. The Crofter's Flask employed people locally who relied on the wages. Rowan Croft was booked up in advance with holiday lets. Now there weren't enough hours in her day and she needed staff, but funds were stretched.

Plus a recent spate of 'problems' with the pub were adding to her headaches. From a freezer that had gone on the blink and cost a fortune for new stock, to a microwave fire that nearly caused a kitchen meltdown. The pub needed tender care and investment. Trouble was Jess had few reserves left to tend to its needs.

As she drove, her thoughts about the pub and its pressures nagging in her mind, Jess was also intensely aware of Gabe Garrett beside her. Big, tall and lean; his presence made her need to gather and calm.

'No hat tonight?' she asked, striving for social chit-chat.

'Trying to blend in. Doubt I'll succeed.'

Jess said nothing but permitted herself a small smile.

'The locals will be delighted to have a newcomer to interrogate. They love a stranger on the radar.'

'Sounds as bad as Tall Trees Creek.' Gabe faked a wince.

Jess couldn't help but notice him flex long fingers over jean-clad thighs.

'In Invergarry, inquisition is a highly developed welcoming technique honed to an art form. They like that in Texas?'

'Newcomers have to earn respect and trust. Guess it's the same most places; small towns the same the world over.'

Somehow — looking like he did — Jess doubted Gabe Garrett could ever blend in.

'I tried your bath soak,' Gabe added, sending a blush at full speed to hijack her complexion. 'Ironed out the travel kinks more than I imagined.' His voice was smokey and his eyes didn't meet hers.

Jess gulped.

'I said I was good, didn't I?' she joked. 'Can't be beaten.'

'Very good. Almost dozed in the bath. Wonderin' if you were trying to drown me?' Gabe looked at her with dark eyes.

'I never drown a guest before they pay the bill.'

Gabe grinned briefly. It crinkled his eyes and showcased white teeth. 'Smarter than you look, though I still think you might slay me discreetly.'

Sadly his smile disappeared as swiftly as it had arrived. Jess figured Gabe Garrett should smile like that more often.

'Why ever would you think such a thing, Mr Garrett?'

'Payback. You're Ruth and Josh's

accomplice. I see through the charm. They've briefed you to give me a good old hard time.'

Something about him made her bubble inside with his unexpectedness. She hadn't anticipated Gabe Garrett to have an approachable or open bone in his body. She'd expected Texas alpha with attitude and no bending, but he wasn't like that at all.

The banter alone was progress. The open distrust was so much healthier than stand-off.

When differences were put aside and he forgot he was in Scotland — he was OK. Though he wasn't forgiven for the wedding woes yet.

'You're right. I'll leave the deed until after the wedding but I'm still thinking up my dastardly method. If you have any preferences let me know. I hardly think herbal remedies goes hand in hand with being a hit woman though, do you?'

His eyebrow rose at her provoking tone. 'I wouldn't put anything past you,

Ms Gilmour. How d'you end up dabbling in remedies anyhow?'

Jess smiled and firmed her fingers on the steering wheel. 'My grandmother used to live in Rowan Croft. She was a herbalist and made soaps and salves from home before she passed away. I still have all her notebooks. Always dreamed of doing it for real, too, but only managed it relatively recently; the shop's my new baby.'

She could already smell the giveaway scent on Gabe's skin; he'd really used it. His eyes caught hers and her complexion heated. He smelled of cedarwood; she knew essential oils like a cab driver knows the short-routes.

Jess kept her eyes on the road and blew out a breath. 'The pub was my husband's but he's no longer here. I was his business manager. Dan wouldn't trust any outsider with jobs involving money. Now he's gone and I run both businesses. It's necessary work. The soap store is my first love but the inn helps me make it all pay.'

Gabe stared at her for some seconds, a young woman who had obviously been through so much.

'I'm sorry about things not working out with your husband, ma'am.'

Jess chose to gloss over the facts. 'He's dead now. Four years on and I have the life I want. Dan and I weren't marriage of the century. Not like Josh and Ruth will be.'

Jess couldn't handle sympathy about a husband she didn't grieve for. It was easier to act like she was separated than admit she was a widow. But when she turned to Gabe he looked taken aback.

'Then I'm sorry for your loss,' he apologised.

She tried a fresh tack and a new topic.

'Should I mention that I heard a rumour that your brother plans to be married in a kilt? Does that mean — as best man — that you'll be sporting one?'

Gabe stared at her then shook his head.

'Not in this lifetime.'

The look on his face made her laugh aloud at his patent horror. Teasing Gabe Garrett was more fun that she'd realised.

'Well that's a shame, Mr Garrett, because I think a kilt might be just what you're in need of to start falling in love with Scotland!' Jess started laughing and in spite of herself pretty soon couldn't stop.

★ ★ ★

Gabe glanced at the woman driving him down twisty highland roads at breakneck speed. He felt like the proverbial tourist; out of his comfort zone.

She kept laughing at him — and some weird sadistic thing inside him liked it!

He'd done nothing but marvel at his new hostess since he'd got here. That was not his usual style. Did altitude sickness have side-effects?

39

Jess was biting her lip — an incredibly attractive habit. He shifted his attention as she changed gears and gunned the accelerator. He wished his brain hadn't freeze-framed pearly teeth against pink lips. He didn't even want to linger on the cornflower blue eyes and long, dusty lashes.

Especially now that he knew she was a widow. And since, as Ruth's best friend, she clearly couldn't stand him. The bad guy Garrett tag must've been discussed locally and it had stuck.

Still, he wished he hadn't bemoaned losing Josh to Jess. Now that she'd confided she was widowed.

'You always drive this fast? Crazed demon with a death wish.' Gabe hoped his knuckles weren't showing white.

'The kitchen's under-staffed. I have a great restaurant rating to maintain. Plus I want to keep the staff I've got.'

'If I'd known you double as a stunt woman I might have walked after all.'

Jess flicked a glance at him then seemed to loosen up. 'Aren't cowboys supposed to be daring?'

Gabe cleared his throat. 'You call g-force acceleration fun?'

Jess rectified a near miss with a large pothole and swerved widely. She had the decency to apply the brake and adjust speed. Still, he wondered if he should've checked his life assurance before leaving.

'Right now there are probably fifteen groups of people waiting. I don't want them banging on tables.'

'Let them wait. And let me live.'

Their eyes met and Jess freely laughed aloud. It did something inside him. Eased out knots of tension; knots he'd held tight for a long time. Since finding out about Mom's illness. Since Marie and all she'd done to his head and insides. Since Josh told them he was leaving too. Since Josh announced he was engaged. Emotions he'd stuffed away and padlocked up. It was the cowboy way — pack the feelings deep and get on with the duties of life.

But since waking up to the realisation

that the sole responsibility of Broken Bridle Ranch was his, come hell or high water, he'd felt different than he'd ever felt before.

Lately Gabe Garrett had realised that nobody wanted his legacy. The Garrett dynasty, once so great and traditions-focused, had dwindled and amounted to a one man ranch with a hired team that was turning into a noose around his neck.

'I know these roads like the back of my hand. You'll get there safely,' Jess assured. 'Stop being so edgy.'

Gabe kept his hand on the door grip. 'You always work three jobs in a day?'

'Keeps me out of trouble. Since I lost my husband I lost the choice. I can grab a sandwich later.'

Gabe found his throat tighten. She'd said it so easily then jumped to talk of sandwiches. She'd lost her lover and survived to tell the tale. What was his excuse for his iron heart?

'I'm so sorry about earlier. Talking about losing my brother. You've clearly had a tougher time than me,' he said.

She batted his words away but didn't answer. Suddenly driving along beside this sassy, attractive woman felt more awkward than ever. Especially when those long lashes didn't fit any widow stereotype at all.

'Can I ask a question?' she said eventually and flicked him a glance.

Gabe nodded.

'I know it's none of my business but why decline the wedding invitation? Sorry if that's direct . . . ' she said. 'I do have you hostage in a speeding vehicle and being behind the wheel makes me gung ho. I figured I'd push my advantage.'

Gabe shook his head. 'It's nothing against your friend; I didn't bargain on losing my brother this way. Scotland's another planet to a guy who rarely leaves his State. I never imagined I'd lose my family links in quick succession. Now that it's happened it's taking me time to adjust.'

'They're very much in love,' Jess said softly.

Only Gabe was a realist not a romantic. 'Love can fade. What if it goes wrong?' he parried swiftly. 'What if he realises he's made a mistake?'

Jess shook her head. 'They're like swans — they'll mate for life. You'll see how deep it goes when they're together. Josh and Ruth are perfect.'

Born romantic, thought Gabe. Crazy talk.

She was a woman who'd lost a husband but who still believed in hearts, flowers and baloney. Unfortunately he didn't. Not since Marie.

'I've seen couples swear undying love. Next minute it's about alimony,' Gabe said with a razor sharp edge to his voice.

Jess knitted her brows. 'They can come for long holidays on your ranch and you can vacation here. You needn't lose each other. Families manage and stick together through thick and thin. Use the internet and send lots of emails. And always hold on to the most special memories. Replay them often; it works.'

'I guess, but I'd rather 'stick together' in Texas.'

Jess looked at him hard and Gabe felt his chest thud.

It felt like he needed to run and punch something hard.

Maybe some families coped — he just hadn't bargained on him and Nancy being the only Garretts left in Texas — and now he felt bad for the things he'd noticed about Jess. Physical details that made a man remember why he was a man.

And Gabe Garrett had enough problems; women had always been a breed he could never understand.

'Let's change the subject,' Jess concluded.

'Can't you hire help? If this was back home I'd be telling my manager to hire extras,' Gabe confided. 'Run on low too long you risk losing control of the reins.'

'The economy's tight and work here is tourist season oriented. I have to be prudent.' Her comments were clipped and her narrowed eyes and straight posture suggested she thought he had no right to comment.

'By doing extreme shifts 'til you drop?' Gabe challenged.

'Actually Josh told me you were the family workaholic. How come you're attacking my work/life balance?'

'I work hard but have a great team as back-up. It's my legacy, a duty I have to uphold.'

He was suddenly uncomfortable thinking about his home town and the emotions his ranch incited. It reminded him that he needed his brother there to help him with decisions. He wanted Josh's sons to grow up as ranchers too.

'All ranchers work hard but I don't let a day go by when I don't recognise how blessed I am to work my family's ranch. A ranch is a family obligation going back generations,' he stated.

Jess turned in her seat to squarely

accuse him. 'And if family's so pivotal then surely it's important that your brother is marrying the woman he loves the most. I want the best for the people I love, however that impacts on me.'

'Meaning you think I'm the selfish one?'

Losing his mother to a beast that stole her away wasn't the best outcome for anyone, let alone a woman he'd loved so dearly. Betsy Mae had been there in body — some days were bearable, others she'd looked at him all memory lost and confusion in its place. Every molecule of him ached for what dementia had done . . . He'd wanted much better for his mother.

Maybe that's why losing Josh was intolerable.

Gabe loved Broken Bridle. Only lately he was grumpy about everything. Even the ranch. Grumpy because life was getting a new ending without his consent, and the buck always rested with him.

Jess blushed but continued. 'Let's not

fight when we've agreed a truce.'

Gabe sounded grim even to his own ears. 'Best to change topic. We both clearly believe strongly in our own views.'

A white painted building nestled on the loch front came into view. It sat in a stunning harbour location — quaint charm amid the rugged beauty of mountains and a stunning loch. Was this how Josh fell for Scotland?

Gabe forced his empathy away. It wasn't Texas. And it wasn't home. It could never come close for him.

He didn't want to be here, he had to keep focusing on that and reminding himself that he was the only one who'd held firm. He was the one in the right here.

'Think you'd have found it?' Jess asked.

'Maybe,' Gabe admitted. 'Not that I'm not grateful for your expertise and your driving skills.'

When she pulled up they got out of the van and Jess's flaxen hair was stirred by the breeze's grasp across the water. It caused the oxygen in his chest to thump inside his windpipe. She was beautiful. Captivating even when ruffled.

Opinionated too — yet although their views differed, somehow he found himself admiring her spunky attitude to life.

'Enjoy your dinner. I know your brother is delighted to have you as his guest,' she said with a forced smile.

Gabe gave a searching stare. 'And take a break, don't go collapsing from exhaustion.' Gabe watched her levelly. 'I hope he's as in love as you say. Don't wanna keep being the bad guy.'

Jess seemed to consider her words. Eventually she said, 'He'll simply be delighted you've come, which makes you a good guy at heart.'

Gabe watched her with intrigue as Jess dashed through the doorway then swept away on silver baseball boots.

A voice called out and broke the

moment. 'Gabriel Garrett as I live and breathe!'

'Josh Nathanial Garrett.' Gabe forced a smile and strode towards his brother.

'Come join us. We've bagged the best tables by the loch.'

Josh said the word 'loch' like a local and immediately Gabe knew this country had changed his brother already. He stood beside a raven-haired woman who must be Ruth, his fiancée. An oval face framed bright blue eyes and an open smile. She was beautiful; he could see why Josh was smitten. Gabe knew his Mom would have wanted to see Josh look this happy.

Emotion welled inside Gabe and he worked to rein it in. The sharp pang of jealously persisted that someone held more power over Josh than their homeland.

He'd lost the war.

He'd never bring him home now.

'I lost the bet; said you'd be wearing the Stetson,' said Josh, nearing his brother and clasping his hand in his own.

Gabe joined his brother and future sister-in-law.

'Stetson's jet lagged. Now what's all this cockamamie about tying the knot in a kilt? It all stops here!'

3

Halfway through kitchen duty, Jess realised an impromptu musical performance was underway in the dining area and all diners were suddenly as impressed by the entertainment as the food.

In high tourist season the pub regularly hired a local musical trio. Angus on fiddle, Stan on accordion and Stella on piano. They played sedate Scottish airs to please the tourists. Tonight the medley was more rousing with strains of Country and Western and an amazing voice to carry them off.

Jess glanced through the serving hatch, grinning. A young female brunette was singing centre stage as the Loch Side Players kept time; such a contrast to their usual style it wasn't true. It wasn't just good — it was wonderful. She stood watching her dining guests enjoying the entertainment.

By the time she'd finished there was applause and rousing chants for more but the pretty chanteuse replaced her microphone with a bow and left with a mouthed thank-you.

Jess called Heather over. 'Who's that singer?'

'Josh's baby sister, Nancy. She'll be singing at the wedding. She's been practising with the band for the big day.'

'I wonder if she'd consider a permanent booking during her stay? Look, everybody loves it!' Jess grinned.

'Doubt it. Texas is a long way to commute. She lives in Tall Trees Creek on her big brother's ranch.'

Jess took a break to go and approach Nancy Garrett before she left.

'Hi,' she said smiling. 'I'm Jess — Ruth's friend. Great to meet you. You're welcome to come sing here any night you like; the customers loved it.'

Nancy's pretty smile grew even more

radiant and she wrinkled her nose in blushed pleasure. 'Great to meet you, Jess. I've heard of you from Ruth already. And about your amazing skincare store; Ruth's converted me to nettle, aloe and green tea cream. I must stock up and take some back home. I have pretty sensitive skin so it'll be a godsend to find something that agrees with me!'

Nancy Garrett was an attractive, engaging young woman. Jess guessed she must be five years or so younger than herself, making her early twenties. She was different to both her brothers and yet she shared similarities — her colouring and the ready sparkle in green eyes.

She smiled at Nancy's compliments. 'How about we trade? Another performance some time, for a healthy supply of cream and bathing products?'

'I'm available whenever you want me; you can even pick the play list. You met my big brother yet? I hope he's playing nice?'

Both Nancy's knowing look and searching enquiry made Jess unsure of how to answer. She chose diplomacy. 'Once he gets to know Ruth he'll love her as much as we all do. Ah . . . speak of the devil.'

Just then Ruth came through the door. 'I'm nominated to bring the boys their drinks,' she whispered. 'And give them some catch up time. I figure I'll give them privacy to bond.'

Nancy raised her brows. 'They just need to talk. It's time to move on. Thing is, Gabe's stubborn as Hennessey's old mule back home. He covers up and digs things way too deep. I'm just glad he came because right until the last minute he was trying to duck out.'

Jess shrugged, wary of how much to reveal and unwilling to comment. 'I know Ruth'll sleep better knowing the family issues are ironed out. And your brother Gabe is a decent guy. Maybe he just needs to feel included?'

Jess looked out of the window, only just managing to discern two tall male figures in the gathering dusk. Privately she was glad for them but Jess also felt her heart shimmy and that surprised her.

She hoped Gabe might manage to find resolution to his deep grievances. She knew the destructive powers of resentment and lack of communication — she'd lived with them throughout her married life.

Jess felt her head heat. It was hot tonight and the ceiling fans didn't seem to be circulating nearly enough air. She pushed the back of her wrist to her forehead.

'Are you OK?' Ruth asked. 'You look beat, Jess.'

'I'm fine. Just busy, I forgot how busy it gets working in the kitchen. Makes me appreciate how hard my staff have to work. Come on, let's get your drinks sorted,' she invited.

Nancy and Ruth followed her to the bar.

★ ★ ★

Gabe watched the birds swooping low on Loch Dinnoch. He could easier fly than find the right words to say to his brother but he'd come this far so he had to give it a try.

His eyes met Josh's in the twilight. 'I was angry at you. We lost Momma and then a month after the funeral you announced you were leaving. Now you aren't comin' back. I feared this could happen and I took my feelings out on you.'

Josh replied softly, 'I'm sorry I went loco. But once you start you just don't listen, Gabe. Always been the same.'

Gabe shrugged. 'I was angry that you felt free enough to go your own way and I never have. Angry that home didn't matter enough to you.'

Both men had opened up the suitcases on their states of mind and were openly airing their feelings. Such clarity was best between brothers. Neither wanted bad feelings to fester.

Josh sighed hard then scanned the mountain across the loch. 'Texas matters and always will. We both said stuff we didn't mean. I came here because after Momma I needed freedom. Now Ruth's the one — plain and simple as it gets.'

Gabe scuffed his boots in the lochside shingle. Sandy fresh water and foliage aromas carried on the night breeze. 'I still figure you're throwing your heritage away but I've no right to veto your life plan, Josh, even if I don't agree with it. I guess we agree to differ and I have to give you my trust.'

Josh stood broad and tall with hands tucked in his back pockets. 'You're the cowboy born and bred, not me. Ruth makes me a better man. It's not a premeditated rejection of you or Tall Trees or any of my past.'

'And I'm sorry we fought,' said Gabe. 'Sorry for the rift.'

Not so much sorry for what he'd said, but sorry that Josh never would come home. Sorry for their impasse.

Josh had always known from youth he'd longed to be a vet and he'd yearned to travel. But he'd ended up in Scotland; working at Ruth's stables. And now he'd set up his own practice and didn't intend to come back at all.

'Is this partly about Marie and Momma?' Josh asked.

Gabe had to resist the urge to yell. It was so much more. And yet it had morphed into something that could suffocate his frail emotions. It was everything; Momma getting ill and him having the hard decisions about her care. Marie planning to marry him then defecting in the final hour.

'Still haven't recovered from losing Mom or from seeing the changes in her. Marie's just ancient history.'

Gabe sighed. 'Our love wasn't strong enough. I opted to stay in Tall Trees and I've stuck by it; proved to be for the best.'

Josh put his arm around his brother's shoulder. 'She wanted you to go to New York and you couldn't commit.'

'Because of Broken Bridle. Because of my responsibilities.'

'Suggesting you think I've broken the cardinal sin?' Josh withdrew his arm and stared hard at his elder brother. 'Josh put himself first. Betrayed the family.'

'I'm not gonna lie — that's how I've seen it for a while. But if you can get over it, I guess I have to. You're your own man.'

There was a long pause as Josh digested his words.

Josh lent his foot against an old fallen log on the lochside. 'I appreciate you being here, Gabe. In time I know you'll see I did the right thing. Ruth and I are for keeps — our love won't falter.'

Gabe tucked his arguments tight. There were still things he wanted to say — like how come Ruth wouldn't consider making a home in Texas? And biggest of all — why did Josh think it was OK to shove responsibilities onto Gabe's shoulders like an iron yoke? Like he'd done with their Momma too.

He couldn't say that now; especially when he saw Ruth's slim silhouette approach and though her smile was bright in the dusky light, he could tell her posture was hesitant.

Gabe chose to blur the truth. 'I'm lucky to watch you tie the knot with the woman you love. It matters to me and Nancy and I've never seen you look happier.'

'I'm marrying Ruth — the most amazing woman I've ever met. Nothing could be better in this world. I'm so glad you're here to witness the wedding,' Josh confided. His expression and the sincerity in his eyes told of the truth of his words.

He and Josh had worked on their fragile brotherly bridge. If only Gabe felt the joy he faked. But no-one recognised his ramping isolation, his lingering doubts, or the personal maelstrom that turned everything around him to indigo blue.

Gabe kept his inner voices quiet and held the most important part of their conversation back.

I miss you already, brother. I'm more alone now than ever.

★   ★   ★

At that moment a startling shout caused the men to turn their attention to the clifftop by the harbour out front of the inn.

The voice was Nancy's and she now stood frantically waving then let out another panicked shout from the railings.

They could hear her call clearly. 'Come, quickly!' It spurred them into action. Ruth followed close behind.

They ran before they heard more. Sprinting, stride for stride, side by side.

As both men tore up the rocky banking, missing the stairs in favour of speed, they heard her garbled explanation. 'Quickly . . . we have to go to her. It's Jess. We need help! She's collapsed! We think she's fainted but she's totally out. And she doesn't look good. She's so pale.'

Nancy's face told of fear and Gabe briefly touched his sister's shoulder as Josh put his hand around his fiancée's to reassure her. They ran swiftly to the pub where concerned onlookers were gathering around the pub door looking grim and worried. They had to push through the crowd of people to access the bar.

Josh threw Gabe a swift glance. Fight or flight reflexes sparked between them like exposed wires. It felt like being back during some crisis at Broken Bridle — the brothers still worked well together even after so long apart. But there was no time for taking solace in working in unison again — Jess needed help fast.

'Let us through,' Gabe declared roughly and the milling crowd dispersed on command. He pushed into the bar area at speed to find Jess lying prostrate on the floor. She was pale, her leg looked as if it was contorted at an odd, uncomfortable angle and for a scary moment Gabe's heart lurched

— he wasn't even sure that she was breathing at all.

⋆ ⋆ ⋆

Jess lay on the floor on the cold, hard terracotta tiles of the Crofter's bar.

When he reached her side he quickly checked for breathing and a pulse. Her pulse was weak but she was, thankfully, breathing.

Gabe couldn't help but notice how her dusty blonde hair was splayed out and her complexion was so very pale; her lips the colour of the palest ice summer roses.

But this was reality and time was of the essence — there were shards of sharp, smashed glass strewn like hazardous jewels around the floor that made him wince. A stark blood stain on Jess's arm and a tiny gash on her cheek attested to their danger.

'She's breathing but her pulse is weak,' Gabe said. 'Someone help clear up the glass as a priority. It's a danger.'

The sight of her blood had caused something to curdle as concern ramped inside Gabe. He longed to turn back the clock and wished he'd been more emphatic in his entreaties for Jess to take it easy.

Why had this happened? Did she have a condition — too many questions he didn't have answers to crowded for attention in his brain.

'Clear the way here, let's have some privacy and some room,' Gabe appealed again, noting that onlookers were still around them.

Josh, right beside him stood up and took over removing spectators from the scene. They'd avoided the shards of smashed glass on the floor and Nancy was right now making an effort to sweep around them and remove fragments wherever she could.

'You OK to do this, brother?' Josh checked over his shoulder.

Gabe nodded. He knew enough medical basics to take the lead. As a veterinarian Josh could take control but

65

Gabe was used to first aid and the occasional medical crises of ranch life.

'I'm fine here. Just placate the guests and keep things calm, people are naturally worried,' Gabe said quietly to his brother who nodded and did his bidding.

'She blanked out?' Gabe asked those nearby as he placed his finger on her pulse point at her neck again, rewarded with a slightly stronger flicker. Her skin felt cool. Her flowery shower-fresh scent assaulted him and brought back instant unbidden images of being close together in the confines of her van. How he wished she was chatty and conscious once more.

His sister Nancy went into a breathy explanation of events for his benefit. 'She was serving drinks. She'd said she was feeling really tired and a bit odd and dizzy but she'd put it down to feeling beat and the kitchen staff situation meant she'd no option but to work. Ruth had just told her that if she wanted a break in a minute, she'd take over. She'd made up drinks for Ruth to take down to you at the loch, then she started serving others in the bar. She stepped on the step stool to reach an optic then fell backwards with the glasses still in her hands.'

Gabe took the reins as he would on the ranch by making Nancy calm down by giving her something to do.

'Fetch a damp cloth quickly so I can clear the last tiny fragments of glass. Thanks for sweeping, that's a great help. Then work on making everyone stay clear with Josh. OK?'

Nancy nodded.

'Has the local doctor been called?' Gabe asked Ruth.

Ruth, worrying at her lip and looking shocked, nodded. 'On his way now after I called. He lives nearby so he won't be long.'

'Good. Smart thinkin'. Well done, Ruth.' Gabe chanced a smile to his sister-in-law-to-be to try to calm her worries. 'Maybe you could check that all's well in the kitchen?'

Just then Jess let out a soft moan and her eyelids began to flutter open which caused hope to leap inside Gabe.

'Wh . . . where am I . . . ?' Jess asked on a ragged croak.

'Welcome back, you've had a nasty fall,' Gabe crooned. 'You had us all worried for a second there.'

Jess's eyes ghosted open then shut again. 'I feel weird.'

'No rush — just lie there and take it easy. I'm just going to sit here and talk to you until you're feeling a little more like yourself.' He slipped his fingers around her wrist to inconspicuously feel for and measure her pulse again, disguising the move by slipping his big hand around hers. She was cold and her hand felt slim and tiny in his. A jolt inside him when her eyes widened and speared his almost knocked him sideways.

He was more worried about Jess Gilmour than he'd realised. She didn't deserve any of this.

Gabe forced a smile. 'Just because I

said you weren't to collapse from exhaustion you didn't have to go and prove me wrong. You gonna go against my wishes all the time I'm here?'

Jess's stared right at him. Her eyes misted with confusion and a generous dose of fear. He saw a tear slip from her eye.

'I'll try not to.'

Gabe stroked the inside of her palm with his fingers. 'You're OK. You're among friends. Now take it easy. Doc's on his way.'

'I'm sorry. I've messed up,' she whispered.

Jess's chin wobbled as she held back tears and Gabe reached out to push back the tendrils of her hair. He blotted the tears with his thumb. 'Now, now. We all have slip-ups occasionally. I told you that before, remember?'

Nancy appeared again with the dustpan and cloth and began to remove the remaining shards, carefully making the area safe.

'You're gonna be just fine,' Gabe told

her in his warmest, honeyed voice. 'Nothin' a bit of time and care and easy relaxation won't fix. And a good decent meal inside you at some point in the future. I'm figurin' you just need to put you first for a change. Sometimes it's hard, but it's essential.'

Jess's eyes held his with unspoken thanks and she nodded.

Gabe visually examined the cuts and reassured himself that they were only minor surface wounds that wouldn't require stitches. 'Ever blacked out like this before, Jess?'

She replied in the negative. Again the haunted look returned to her eyes. She was freaked out and frightened. Hardly a big surprise.

Gabe felt something inside his heart shift with the sheer impact of their situation — the proximity? The predicament? Or the magnetic charm of the woman beside him? Maybe those stunning blue eyes looking deep into his soul?

'You told me to be careful,' she

whispered softly.

Gabe tried his best to grin at her. 'And now I have you here at my mercy I want you to listen carefully. Stop talking. Take it easy. Ease up on yourself — especially when you're blacking out all over the place. You intending to keep falling into my arms the whole time I'm here? Much as I enjoy the knight in shining armour role, I'd rather you just did it the subtle, healthy way.'

Jess seemed to find it hard to swallow.

'Now, how's the bump on the head feeling?'

'Head is fine. I think I may've turned over on my ankle though, feels like I twisted it. One minute I was serving, next I just keeled over. Think I'm the worst hostess in the world?'

Gabe shook his head. He wished he didn't still have an anxious pounding inside him that was making him worry about the slightly glazed look in Jess's eyes and the slight clamminess of her skin. Though if she had twisted and sprained her ankle it could well be pain coming to the fore.

Just then a new face appeared in the crowd — a dark blond haired, muscular man in a plaid shirt with a big black bag in his hand. He held a stethoscope.

'I'm Ben Logan, the local doctor. Allow me access to the patient please?'

Gabe moved away, letting go of Jess's hand reluctantly. But Ben Logan had an air of calm efficiency and pragmatic authority, so he was the best man for the job.

'Hi honey,' he heard Ben say to his holiday-let landlady. 'I've missed you. The thing's you'll do to get my attention, hmm?'

Ben immediately smoothed away Jess's hair from her temple and squeezed her hand then gently touched her lips with his finger. Gabe saw the move and felt unnerving rumblings swell inside him. Half of him itched to shout at the guy to back up. Half of him wished he'd done that when he'd had the chance. But the wild instincts were swiftly snuffed by the situation.

Ben caught his gaze. 'Could you concentrate on crowd control? Maybe see everyone out of the pub in a calm and orderly fashion?'

'I'll cover that for you,' Gabe muttered, feeling like he'd just been delegated from head rancher to bunk-house boy in a blink.

Something told him Ben was more than just her doctor. Why did that bother him so? Why did the romantic affairs of a woman he'd only just met jar inside him?

The best thing to do was focus and act — ranch mantra. Cowboy's code.

'Right Josh, Ruth and Nancy — here's the plan. We'll ask folks to kindly vacate without settlin' bills. The decent ones'll pay anyhow. The ones who don't will be on my private 'hunt 'em down for threats list'. So everybody — let's get to it.'

★　★　★

When Jess got back from hospital she was shattered, but patched up and relieved — if confused.

Her arm was now in a sling because her wrist had been hurt and her ankle — sprained not broken — was in a supportive bandage with a doctor's firm order to rest up. Ben — Dr Logan — had taken her to hospital and stayed while she was seen to at the minor injuries department.

Though now she was glad to be back home. Rowan Croft, Bramble Bank and her own home, Otter's Cottage, sat in darkness. Her Pure Pleasures shop looked strange and empty and dark at this early hour of the morning.

A stray owl's hoot heralded their arrival when Ben switched off his jeep's engine and turned to their passenger in the back.

Gabriel Garrett sat darkly and silently stiff, like a chaperone. A brooding hulk of a cowboy who'd cleared out her restaurant, marshalled her clients into paying with cool charm and had then stayed throughout the whole hospital ordeal. She'd told him to go — he hadn't listened.

Ben's expression told of waning patience.

'It was good of you to stay with Jess at the hospital, Mr Garrett, but it really wasn't necessary. Thank you, but I'll deal with the patient from here.'

Jess felt too tired, freaked out and confused to work out if the slightly irritated edge to Ben Logan's voice was real or imagined.

Or maybe he was miffed at having to come out and spend hours of his free time with her at the local hospital thirty miles away. After all, it was stretching his interest now that they were no longer dating.

He'd wanted to date her for a while a few months back. Now he'd moved on, thanks to her rebuffs, and she hadn't seen him for a month at least. With Ben she'd sensed he would've liked more and a faster journey to a romantic entanglement she just didn't feel ready to commit to.

Ben was nice; he was decent. Unfortunately, he was also boring and not her type. If Jess, obsessed by business and concocting new bathing aids and soap mixes, had a type at all that is.

Gabe's western US drawl rumbled in answer from the back seat. 'Call it the cowboy code Dr Logan — where I'm from we see the job through,' Gabe answered. 'I wouldn't dream of leaving my landlady alone. Figured I had a responsibility.'

She heard the car door click as he climbed out and then opened her door in a gentlemanly fashion for her. Had he done it just to rile Ben, Jess wondered?

'She wasn't alone. She was with me,' Ben snapped back. 'And she's with me now. What I'm trying to say is, thanks for your time and patience.'

Ben had circled the car quickly and was now by Gabe's side trying to elbow him out of the way.

They stood shoulder to shoulder bristling with manhood and irked responsibility.

Jess resisted the urge to groan and to make matters worse, they both looked at her, vying to be the chosen one to offer her assistance from the car.

'How about I try this myself,' Jess said and gripped onto the door handle. 'It'll be good practice,' she answered. 'And you've done way too much already, Ben. I'm fine on my own and you'll have a surgery to handle early in the morning. Please, go now. I can't thank you enough — I owe you an on-the-house meal at The Crofter's for all your help.'

Ben glared at Gabe like he was considering a swift felling punch.

'Let me at least show you to your door. I'm sure Mr Garrett will be jet lagged.'

Jess wanted to scream. Or tell them to take a hike.

From embarrassing fainting incident

— the hospital had taken bloods and had given her a lecture on doing too much and not taking sufficient breaks — to men virtually duelling for her attentions. It was all too much. She intended to put a stop to this now.

It was nice to have two chivalrous men try to assist you but when they started point scoring like she was a prize suckling pig it had to be stopped.

'Ben — go home now. And Gabe — see me to my door and then get inside yourself. I fainted; it wasn't a major incident. I just need to get inside and rest. No biggie.'

Ben glowered with a look like thunder and hands on hips. 'I'm not sure . . . '

Jess began to limp away anyway. 'I'm doing my own thing, Dr Logan.'

Gabe came to her side and gave her his arm.

'I'll be back later tomorrow with blood test results,' Ben assured her.

Gabe saluted to the miffed doctor.

'I'll make sure she's ready to receive you.'

Jess tried to placate him. 'Then I'll see you tomorrow, Ben. Looking forward to it.'

Ben nodded and seemed somewhat pacified.

'OK. But no taxing yourself. Tomorrow you take it easy — even if you do have a guest. I'm sure Mr Garrett can tend to his own needs for a few days.'

'A born survivor,' Gabe said, putting Jess's good arm more fully through his own. 'Can cope in the desert on a dry crust if needs be. Rest assured, Dr Logan, we ranch boys know how to rough it.'

Jess resisted the urge to laugh. Gabe was rubbing Ben's nose in this situation and he knew it. She threw him a chastening glare.

'Just take me to the door, open the lock and put the lights on, Gabe, then your chivalry is complete,' Jess said loudly so Ben would hear.

Seconds later the doctor's car door

slammed and the engine started. They watched his lights flash on and the jeep circled before exiting.

Jess whispered darkly, 'You've only been in Invergarry half a day and you've made an enemy. I hope you don't need treatment while you're here or he may insist you suffer unaided.'

'Never could resist an open challenge. Should I be worried that your boyfriend doesn't like me?' Gabe asked.

His chin tilted out in defiance. He didn't look remotely scared of Ben Logan or any man for that matter. And a part of her secretly warmed to that fact.

Jess shook her head. 'We dated once but he's not my boyfriend. I can take care of myself. Usually I do.'

'Not in those jeans?' Gabe countered with the sly accusing look. 'Gonna sleep like a cowboy in denims tonight? You'll need help to get outta those.'

'Not from you and it's none of your concern.' Jess wished her cowboy cottage guest wasn't so smart, so fast or half so deadly handsome. She wished she had a better smart-ass answer and less compulsion to go beet red at his astuteness.

'Denim's great for work wear — but bed wear not so much,' Gabe whispered. 'I'm also very good at tucking in.'

Was he mocking her? Jess narrowed her eyes. 'If you imagine for a second that I'll let you take my jeans off, then you've another thing . . . '

Forsaking all further back-chat Gabe picked her up in strong arms in seconds. 'Cowboys take action. Just mighty glad you're feelin' up to the attitude again. Guess it's a good sign.'

'If you dare to think you're helping me undress you'll be out on your ear by morning,' Jess answered as blushes consumed her as the humiliating end to a bad day.

His green eyes twinkled with amusement in the darkness. 'I don't act where I'm not wanted, Ms Gilmour. Just worried about you handling stairs solo and getting to your room safely without another blackout.'

He did have a point. She had a flight of stairs to climb to her small but cosy and girly attic room. But being in it, with a brawny, hunky rancher was another story . . .

There was a firmness in Gabe's expression when he switched on the hall-light. Though he kept his gaze on the way ahead as he closed the door with her still in his arms. 'Argue all you like but you know I'm right, Miss Jessica.'

'You make me feel like a damsel in a film.'

'Then lay back and enjoy the moment, darlin'.'

He carried her upstairs in easy strides whether he had her consent or not. As they neared her bedroom Jess felt embarrassment mount and wondered if she should have kept Dr Logan as her ally? Being here, being so intimate with a stranger, felt intolerable to a born survivor like Jessica Gilmour.

But with little ceremony Gabe carried her towards her bed and set her down then Gabe disappeared and returned holding a pair of scissors. He switched on her bedside light and laid them on the table.

'You can remove your own jeans if you need to, ma'am. Figure they'll make useful work rags since you won't accept help removing them. I'll be back to bring your coffee in the morning. Now get some rest — I'll lock the door when I leave. Want me to see you to the restroom?'

Jess shook her head and thanked him in a quiet whisper.

Gabe fingered a Stetson hat that wasn't there. 'Then I'll bid you goodnight. Sweet dreams, Jessica Gilmour.'

As Gabe closed the door behind him, Jess reflected that her cowboy guest was completely full of surprises.

And he'd shocked her — man-handled her — but impressed her more than she'd imagined too.

4

Next morning Jess's heart sank as she stared crestfallen from her bedroom window. The pallet of boxed delivery goods rivalled their locally-famed mountain backdrop — large, insurmountable, challenging.

Her usual delivery man always came at ten on the dot. He usually stayed and helped her unload supplies into her storeroom. As if managing with an arm in a sling and a bandaged ankle wasn't bad enough — now she had a dumped and abandoned delivery in her gravel yard to contend with.

Even if she hadn't sprained an ankle and hurt her wrist, even with a motorised barrow, it would take her hours to shift it all. And right now she was far from able to do that. Also she'd had a restless night.

Jess blamed the fainting episode

— she also blamed a cowboy's words . . . A cowboy's teasing smiles and come-to-bed green eyes . . .

Her dreams had involved a faceless stranger wearing denim . . . Jess pushed the thoughts away.

But then her gaze reluctantly roamed to Rowan Croft. Would Gabe be awake? Would he help her again? Was it an imposition to ask it? It was becoming an unhappy habit but she had a long list of jobs and a delivery bodge-up to unravel now. She sighed. She'd never stooped to asking paying guests for help before.

Jess went to her wardrobe, picked out some loose combat trousers and a T-shirt and decided to go and sort out her to-do list. One task at a time was the only way to go.

*   *   *

Just as Jess was examining the stock sheet Gabe came out of the cottage into bright morning sunshine. He sipped a mug of coffee and was holding another. When he reached her, he handed her the mug with a smile.

'Good mornin' ma'am. Will a coffee sweeten your mood today? Fine weather we're havin'.'

Jess would've loved to listen to that accent in replay. But she couldn't admit that. Instead she played the tough, busy, business-owner instead.

'Good morning, Mr Garrett. And I hope you slept well?'

'Sorry,' he shrugged broad, manly shoulders clad in a chambray shirt and teamed with inky dark jeans. 'I meant to rise before you. Think I promised you morning coffee, but I meant in bed. This isn't what I'd call resting up,' he said, stretching long muscular limbs that made her throat dry.

Anyone would think she hadn't seen a man around the place before. Well, she'd had Dan. But somehow Gabe Garrett only magnified her ex-husband's deficiencies.

Was it Gabe's body that made her

feel so jittery around him — or his glances? The fact he looked like he saw too much . . .

Jess yanked her faculties together to reply. 'Thanks for the coffee but I've a business to run whatever Ben Logan's medical advice might be. I can't just shut up shop on a whim.'

Gabe motioned to her bandaged foot. 'Any better?'

'I'm fine.' Jess hoped she sounded more convincing than she felt.

'That's good to hear,' Gabe answered. 'But I have a suggestion: why don't I call my sister around here. A pair of extra hands in your store today won't go amiss.'

'For a minute there I thought I was the one in charge of running things,' Jess replied. As much as it might be intended to be thoughtful, Gabriel Garrett had an unhappy knack of making her feel out of her depth and distinctly lacking — and that was Jess's own personal bête noir.

'As lovely as your sister is — I met

her last night and she's a fabulous singer and a lovely woman — I don't think we need spoil her vacation,' Jess replied.

'Given that it's usually Nancy who's the one bossin' me around, I figure she owes me some favours. It honestly won't be an imposition.' Gabe's jaw flexed. His hands, clearly visible when he took steady sips from his coffee mug, were large and bronzed. Capable hands. He was clearly a man who rallied, who mucked in and who got things done, making him the polar opposite to her ex-husband.

'Thank you for your help yesterday. Thanks for coming to the hospital and being so gentlemanly,' Jess said, feeling the need to broach yesterday's drama without making too big a deal of it.

'Not a problem. The least I could do. A lot of people care about you, Jess, and they were worried.'

'Well, I'm fine now. So there's really no reason to worry.' Jess didn't make eye contact and concentrated on sipping coffee, grateful for the caffeine perk. She still hadn't had much time to think about her fainting spell; it wasn't something she'd ever done before. She guessed Ben might be able to shed more light on it later.

'You managed to speak to your brother last night?' Jess altered topic purposefully.

Gabe nodded then sighed. 'Yes. And he and Ruth do seem mighty loved-up and happy, hard as it is for me to admit it. Here was me thinking I could blow them apart with my big bad brother act! But Ruth was a trooper when you weren't well. She was in a high ol' state and wanted to come to the hospital too.'

Jess smiled. 'I love Ruth right back. Glad the air's cleared with you and Josh.'

'Now back to you,' Gabe drawled. 'And what about my suggestion to recruit some help? That way you can sit back and just tell us all what to do.'

Jess shook her head. 'I'll be right as

rain. It's today's workload that's pressing on my mind.' She nodded to the stacked pallet. 'This isn't the usual arrangement.'

Gabe stood over her, shielding her from the sunshine. 'You look like you need a big strong guy to handle it. Now wherever could you find one of those?' His grin told her he was teasing — and loving it. 'I really don't think you're up to the challenge of this little lot yet.'

Jess sighed deeply. 'They sent a new delivery man this morning. The guy cut and run before I could even use sad eyes and a big ankle bandage to worm a hole in his conscience.'

Gabe sat on the deck; his legs so long she couldn't help notice. His boots were new, not desert scuffed. This rancher was polished — as well as thoughtful. He smiled slowly then said softly, 'I know a big strong ranch guy who could make it better in no time. And be pretty grateful for the manual task. It's been a while since he had a workout.'

Jess's temple furrowed at the words. Firstly, because she liked to rely on herself and wasn't great at accepting charity. Secondly, because she'd known a man who was fitness obsessed before — his name was Dan and he'd been her husband. But Dan had only wanted fitness to preen his looks — not improve his fitness or stamina. The scowl at the way her thoughts had taken a turn for the dark must've shown.

'You OK? Not in any pain again?' Gabe checked. Gabe laid his mug on the deck and stretched those bronzed long muscular arms. Jess tried not to ogle. Or blush. 'I'll phone Josh to do it for you,' he said finally. 'He needs the exercise.'

She smiled at his teasing and narrowed her eyes in warning. 'At least you admit it's too much for you. What a great idea, Josh won't mind helping out I'm sure . . . '

Gabe stalled her with a strong, warm hand. 'A joke. Of course I can handle this. On to it as soon as I finish my coffee. But first we have some things to discuss.'

'You're a guest.' Jess shook her head. 'I'll go make you breakfast. Don't touch anything at all.'

Gabe kept the stalling hand right where it was. 'I said we need to talk. Breakfast can wait. What I want to hear is that you intend to sit right here on this porch today, or on a stool inside your store — no trying to carry on as usual, young lady. That's an order not a warning. My sister Nancy is also being summoned to come and I won't hear a word to contradict that.'

'And how else am I to run my business?' Jess said. OK, she was pouting like a huffy toddler but she did have her pride.

Gabe shrugged. 'I can help. So can Nancy. We'll muddle through until you're fit enough to cope.'

'It's only a sprained ankle. A bruised wrist.'

'And Gabe's orders are never dis-obeyed.'

'So I'm beginning to appreciate. That Stetson hat hides a great big head that thinks it can bark all the orders.'

Gabe surveyed the piled high pallet of goods as he rolled up his shirt sleeves. Jess tried to yank her tongue into action at the grand view of his biceps but failed.

'And once I've done this I'll fix us both breakfast; I'm good in the kitchen too. What do you fancy — an omelette, or eggs Benedict?'

'No.' Jess did a skedaddle gesture with her fingers. 'You seem to be forgetting that you're the guest here.'

Gabe nailed her with eyes as green as the abundant garden foliage outside Rowan Croft. 'Weren't you the one telling me yesterday that in Invergarry I'm among friends? Works both ways. Plus, I thrive on manual labour; I need the exercise. Sedentary livin' dulls a ranch boy's instincts.'

Was protesting good sense or hurt pride? By the look of him he was well equipped for the job — or any job

— but most especially a manual one. She'd quite like to just sit and watch and appreciate. Truth be told, she'd quite like to enjoy the view.

An unexpected quiver of longing sneaked right through Jess as Gabe moved to pick up a weighty box. Years of gym work had never given Dan muscles like those. She shoved her nose deep into her coffee mug and gulped down too hot coffee.

'You're showing off, Garrett,' she muttered.

'Of course. Female audience. Gotta perform for kicks.' Gabe winked and her heartbeat kicked hard. 'All cowboys know how to work the crowd. First rule of rodeo.' Gabe hefted the box and shrugged as if it was feather-light. 'Meal last night was sensational — meant to give you my compliments before you went and dramatised the evening all on your own. But if you were a ranch hand I'd be having the 'slow down or you'll blow it' conversation.'

'Big ranch boss talk. What makes you

think I'll listen?' Jess tried not to smile.

Gabe fake glowered. Her tummy quivered.

'Drink your coffee and watch a real cowboy in action. Some women would pay to see this back home.'

★　★　★

'Are there any jobs in Invergarry you don't sideline in? Just out of interest . . . ' Gabe asked her later after they'd eaten a full Scottish breakfast.

He'd made it, insisting she stay fully out of the kitchen.

He'd also worn her apron and he'd cooked the eggs just the way she liked them without her even asking.

When it came to the boxes he had broken a sweat — only just. It suited him very much. He'd also made a five star class breakfast complete with coffee, orange juice and lashings of toast. And he'd just called his sister Nancy who was due to arrive soon.

Jess tried to ensure her attention

stayed away from the tiny V beneath Gabe's Adam's apple that still had a glisten of perspiration she was trying not to stare at.

Was she crazy? Always watching him, noticing little details that made her goosebump. Most likely the doctor was right; she needed recuperation time. She was just having a 'hero complex' moment because Gabe had so admirably played her knight in shining armour the night before.

In truth she was trying to conceal how incredibly much he was bothering her. How incredibly mad she was at herself. For working this hard and still feeling like a failure. For feeling like a fool because a stranger and a guest felt they had to point it out. Last night he'd warned her she was pushing it — as Ruth had, too — and she'd gone and had a fainting spell instead of listening to anyone at all.

Lesson learned.

Her internal disappointment with herself reminded her of her days with Dan. Being told what to do. Expected to nod and agree and never dare to say, 'Wait a minute, don't I have a say in any of this too? As your wife? As a vital part of this business?'

But no. Dan hadn't wanted democracy or input. He'd wanted a backroom business brain. When they'd married she hadn't realised he'd had more of an eye on her qualifications than her charms as a future wife, to the point that he had secrets padlocked behind his perma-air of autonomy. She'd only found out the truth when his death had hit like a bolt from the blue.

Gabe watched her and shook his head as he removed her plate and took them to wash up in her tiny kitchen sink just off the shop's workshop. 'Soap-making. Store-keeping. Vacation let host which involves cleaning and changing linens and running after guests. Ad hoc chef at The Crofter's kitchen — I should add a kitchen that does a mean trade. That place was packed and yet there you were making bistro meals like it's what you do in tea-breaks. What next — undertaking? Grave digging? You gonna tell me you sideline in being the local windmill operator and mail woman too?'

'I can add a penalty to your bill for unwelcome lecturing,' Jess said, trying to conclude the conversation. 'You can give it up now and lay easy on me. I'm an invalid after all.'

'You did it to me last night; told me exactly what you thought. And I listened, sort of. You told me I needed to consider my duty to my brother and put the grudges aside. It worked. So I guess you were right — there, see, I'm man enough to admit it. Are you woman enough to realise you're going to have to slow up or you'll jeopardise more than your businesses, you'll risk your health too.'

Jess blushed crimson.

Was it anger, frustration or deep,

deep disappointment that fuelled the blushes? Yes, he was right. But that didn't make her like it. Or feel comfortable admitting that she was treading water and not doing a very good job of it either.

Gabe carried on. 'Sometimes a lecture's needed — when your routine isn't good for your health.' His gaze could've turned her bones to jelly.

'And you're qualified to judge?'

'As a matter of fact, I think I am. I run a ranch. I have the welfare of twenty five men to consider. Sometimes that means taking them aside and telling them how I see it.' Gabe bristled. The stark dark line of his brows and the look in his piercing eyes told her he meant every word.

'But you yourself are never wrong?' Jess pushed.

'Didn't say that, ma'am. I'm human, of course I'm wrong sometimes. But I have a good instinct when it comes to people around me.'

She was well aware that the bags

under her eyes were more like luggage. She would laugh but the laugh would crack. Humour couldn't cover the fact that she trying to keep afloat in deep and dangerous depths. Trying to do way too much solo.

She ached everywhere. All she thought about recently was a day off for a lie-in — doing nothing but sleeping away her weariness.

Gabe reprimanded her yet again. 'You're burning the candle at so many ends there's gonna be a blaze.'

'And what do you propose I do about that? Life mentoring. Just what I need.' She shoved her head in her hands.

His green eyes bored into hers and pleaded with her better judgement to listen up. When he looked at her like that she was well aware of the internal inferno; an inferno of attraction. Raw desire at having this man notice when no-one else did.

Gabe shrugged. 'I'm here for three weeks. So is my sister. We could help

— give you breathing space.'

His biceps flexed, sheathed in the tight checked fabric of his shirt. In it he looked way hotter than she'd even suspected yesterday when he'd caught her and his touch hinted at latent rugged strength. 'I'm allowed to give you advice in return for yours, surely? Maybe you can gimme some guidance on mending things with my brother and new sister-in-law in return?'

A pause hung between them.

It took a man to admit it when he was wrong, and Gabe was admitting he'd made errors about Ruth.

Jess sighed. Was this also laced with strong emotional blackmail too? And maybe she didn't want help or intervention — but would rejecting it smack of being as stubborn as Gabe had been? Her mind flew to Nancy and the warnings she'd given about her big brother.

'The store is getting established,' Jess explained. 'The holiday let business came to me when my grandmother passed away. Running it all is tricky but I've no choice. And when I tried to sell The Crofter's, I couldn't find a buyer. I don't have many options right now and I'm not closing the soap store down when I fought so hard to start it up. So I have to just weather the busy times, I guess.'

Gabe strode over to stand beside her. He crouched down. 'If you can't sell the bar then find a manager. I run a ranch and I know killing yourself won't help business. You've nothing to prove but something has to give.'

'And — pardon me for asking — but did I ask you to interfere?'

Gabe stared. 'Ruth is worried. She told me you never get a break. You keeled over last night remember. It's clear you do need some time to recover here.'

'One night in Invergarry and you're suddenly an expert?'

Gabe shook his head at her rebuffs. 'Even Josh says your work schedule is punishing and he's a vet who works regular on-call nights. You need to take care, Jessica.'

Jess pushed her fingers to her temples — difficult with her heartbeat jack hammering in her veins because everyone was ganging up. And he'd called her Jessica; nobody had ever called her that except her dear, beloved grandmother. Hearing it said in a soft, caring tone made her inexplicably itch to cry.

It was nice of everyone to worry, but it was hurtful and it made her feel weak, too. Didn't they realise how vital it was that she prove herself after Dan had left a bitter wound that needed reconstruction? She so desperately wanted to pull off Pure Pleasures in her grandmother's memory.

To get over the past, over Dan . . .

He'd cheated — something she'd been oblivious to until she found the proof in his personal effects. While she'd been running Dan's businesses, he'd been enjoying fringe benefits from his mistress. She worked hard because it shut out the betrayal and diminished self worth.

But beneath the work ethic, disappointment, inadequacy and foolishness still hung heavy as an iron cloak with spikes. It was easier to shove your nose in work than analyse things at a deeper level.

'You're mad now. Mad at me,' Gabe said, a muscle ticking in his jaw.

'Oh, no. I love looking like an idiot and feeling helpless. They're my specialist subjects.'

She scuffed her plastic slip-on beach sandal — the only one that could easily accommodate her bandaged ankle — like a confused schoolgirl. 'In summary I'm a rubbish businesswoman treading water. I can't even see where I'm getting it wrong.'

'You cook like a gifted chef. You have a wonderful holiday cottage business that's spotless and anybody would love to stay at. You make soaps and face creams that I've heard have waiting lists. You really think you're deficient?'

Jess stared at Gabe, bowled over by

what he'd just said.

She wasn't used to compliments. Or indulging her ego. All she could do was blush.

'Don't ever think I'm being unkind. You've plenty of accomplishments.' Gabe's neck was corded. 'You're talented, your business has taken off. You've kept the pub afloat and well frequented during difficult circumstances which tells me you've a good business head. And without your help I'd never have gotten through patching up with Josh. Without your opinions and gentle encouragement I'd be heading back to Texas now. I'm returning the favour.'

Jess looked at him in open shock.

'You work with cattle — have you inherited bull stubbornness too?' she countered.

Gabe grinned widely and then, just when she thought he couldn't, he grinned some more.

'See. I knew you liked me really.'

He'd just nursed and tended the

wounded patch in her self-esteem in a matter of simple sentences — and he could still manage to make her laugh.

'Thank you,' she answered hesitantly. 'Even though you're a big ol' bully.'

'So take my help. Take my advice too. Take me out for dinner as a thank you if you like.'

'Don't push it, Garrett.'

Seconds later his hands were on her arms to pull her up to standing. She smiled up at him and let him pull her towards him. But as they stood body to body a live static charge was her instant reward. It zapped her insides and left her literally reeling.

She wasn't as immune as she liked to pretend. Their eyes connected; they both saw heightened awareness reflected back in each other's eyes.

And then it seemed to happen much too quick. Jess was encircled by strong, sun-warmed arms. She was too close to his large, male body. She could smell his shower-fresh scent and she was looking up at him in surprise and then his mouth was close to hers. Too close.

Gabe Garrett's lips were parted and his head lowered. His firm, full lips touched hers like a whisper, his face close . . .

Jess backed up so swiftly she nearly lost her balance. 'Don't. That wouldn't be a good idea for either of us. I'm in enough of a mess right now.'

'Uh . . . sorry,' Gabe answered softly. 'Signal failure.' He pulled back in confusion and swept a hand through his hair that left it on end, tousled and sexier yet. 'Sorry ma'am,' he replied gruffly.

Unsteady, Jess looked around for something to lean on. Gabe yanked a stool out from the counter for her. She needed a steadying influence after the seismic chemistry that had just erupted out of the blue.

What on earth was wrong with her — where had her usual composure and control fled to?

'Hey guys — here I come! For my

first day in selling delicious soaps.'
Nancy Garrett was riding towards them
on a pink pushbike that Jess recognised
as Ruth's. Thank heaven she hadn't
arrived a minute sooner.

For stalled seconds Gabe and Jess
simply avoided looking at each other
knowing a kiss had been imminent and
possible. And desired ... by both
parties. Big mistake.

Now Gabe was breathing hard while
she was reeling inside like a skittle on a
bowling lane.

'Want my advice? Get out of here
and spend some time with your brother
today,' Jess said. 'Nancy and I will
manage the store. You should go and
indulge in some brotherly bonding.'

Their near kiss still caused her
insides to warm up and shimmy. What
must it be like to have a man who cared
and valued you, desired you too? One
who treated you with respect? Jess
shoved it away hard and bit her lip.

'Got some shears, a hedge trimmer
around this place?'

'I said ... I can manage. Go see Josh.' Jess looked back surprised. 'Tools are in the store-shed. Keys on the hook by the shop backdoor. What are you planning to do with them?'

He scowled and his expression was dark. 'Make myself useful and get out of your hair as requested,' he answered.

'Hey,' Jess welcomed Nancy. 'Great to see you.'

'How are you, Jess? You're looking better than the last time I saw you.' Nancy grinned. She'd dismounted her bike by the porch. 'I'm delighted to come and help. I have a secret yearning to know all about soap-making. It's like a wish come true helping in the store. I feel like a kid in a candy store!'

'Have a look around. Just don't go eating any of the goods or you'll be the one in need of medical help!'

'Ignore my brother,' said Nancy, nearing Jess and plopping her garish lime green tasselled handbag on the countertop. 'He's always grouchy as a bear with a cactus wound in the mornings. He gets better by dinner time. Most of his ranch hands have honour degrees in diplomacy and keeping a low profile.' She winked at her brother affectionately.

Luckily with a shrug and a sigh Gabe stomped off before they could share more awkward moments, or Nancy could detect any hot, palpable friction in the air between them.

Jess called out to him just before he disappeared from view. 'Yes, I'll consider hiring help. But I don't want you hanging around here bossing me around. A big man can lift boxes. A real man does the right thing — even when it's hard. Go see Josh today. Stop being stubborn and listen back.'

'Stubborn isn't the worst of me,' she heard Gabe mumble. 'When I put my mind to something, I make sure good sense prevails.'

Nancy grinned and gave Jess a thumbs up.

'Hey. You're gonna be a good influence on Grumpy Gabriel. Nice work! He's just done a running scared act and that hardly ever happens! Kudos, Jess.'

'Come through,' Jess urged. 'Let me show you around and how this place works before opening time.'

5

Jess sat at her office desk and flicked through pages she'd just designed for her Pure Pleasures website. The new ranges filled her with quiet accomplishment and the website was good considering it was as homemade as her soaps.

After a day where she'd sat on a stool behind the shop counter and done very little while the Garretts took the reins — it was good to do something for herself for a change.

Gabe had started working wonders outside the store in the grounds and gardens; Nancy had become a beaming ray of sunshine with able hands within. People took to Gabe's vibrant young sister; she had a saleswoman's charm and a genuine apparent affection for the wares which made Jess like her even more.

Secretly she felt guilty for commandeering their time but Gabe wouldn't take any approaches from her to cool it and she and Nancy were having too much fun for her to doubt the situation for too long.

She'd skilfully tried to keep out of Gabe's way — which she'd succeeded in. Except when Dr Ben Logan dropped by with the news that she was badly anaemic with a low red cell blood count. He'd prescribed iron and a green leafy diet plus a few days rest.

Jess sent her pages to be published and nodded at the finished effect. She'd once gone on a couple of web design day courses to help promote Dan's businesses. Now the admin skills were paying off. She didn't mind being back-room girl so much now that creativity took centre stage.

A knock snatched her attention to the door where Gabe now stood in silhouette in the dusky light.

Jess found that her breath caught at his presence even through glass. Not that she'd admit it even to herself. After all there had been the awkward 'near kiss', hadn't there? It was so much better to evade the subject and not think about it, than to sit and brood and consider what it had actually meant.

He'd been out at The Crofter's Flask for supper — and no doubt putting all local minds at rest about her state of health. She'd been secretly glad that he'd made himself busy and they'd kept at a distance. Only now she had to face him again — at night, in her dimly lit office.

Jess tucked back her messy hair and rose to flick on the porch light and beckoned him in.

'Hello Gabe. Good dinner I hope?'

'Not as good as when you made it.'

'Now you're just flattering me.'

She saw him hold a takeaway bag aloft. 'And I've brought something to make sure you don't go without. Doctor's orders, remember?'

'After this morning's mammoth Garrett-cooked breakfast, I had a salad tonight and it was fine. I'm good.'

'About earlier — I'm sorry we quarrelled.'

'Don't mention it,' she answered. 'I think we both like things done our own way.'

Gabe fixed her with a chastening look. 'Ben Logan asked that I make sure you're eating and resting. And since I figure he may come after me with a pitch-fork if I don't do my duty, I now have my honour to uphold. Just doing my job! There's a steak for that red cell count, potatoes and green veggies and chocolate brownie deluxe as a reward — I hear dark bitter chocolate is great for iron. So this is on prescription. Plus I think the cook has your plight on his conscience! Extra helpings.'

Gabe strode to her desk and began decanting his bag of goodies carefully, one foil container after another.

'If I eat all that I'll get fatter than one of your cattle.'

Gabe shook his head. 'Hardly, as I

said — you're taking care of your health. Sit down. There's cutlery. Want a plate — being a refined lady and all?'

'In the cupboard by the sink,' Jess pointed and he retrieved it. He poured her a drink from a bottle of sparkling water from the bag and added lemon from another bag.

'Bon appetit!' he said, flicking a napkin for her and nodding for her to start eating.

'You ever consider being a waiter?' she asked mockingly.

'No, but I do love to be a good host. I'm the barbecue king back home in Tall Trees — with the T-shirt to prove it.'

Jess found herself smiling at that thought. 'How was your meal tonight?'

'I think Heather is trying to sweeten me up. Tonight it was seconds of Death By Chocolate. She's making it her mission for me to have every dessert on the menu. Everyone's sending regards and good wishes. There are three bouquets of flowers outside the door

— I'll put them in vases now.' He went to retrieve them.

'That's lovely but they shouldn't have,' Jess said genuinely touched.

'Maybe they care? Ever consider that?'

'People are kind,' Jess concluded. 'As for Heather — maybe she's sweet on you? I won't tell her husband if you don't. He's a farmer; a pretty big guy. Tosses cabers at Highland Games. Watch out.'

Gabe grimaced. 'From now on I'm a dessert-free zone.'

Jess laughed and began to tuck in. 'This is delicious.'

Gabe retrieved the flowers — which were gorgeous — and began to take them from their wrappings. 'Any vases?'

'One vase. And a bucket and ceramic jug over in the closet.' Gabe retrieved them and set about the task.

'I'm fixing you with my forceful stare because yet again I find you working at way past 'put it away' time. I thought yesterday was proof you need to ease up.' Gabe watched her, his fiery green eyes zapping inside her.

With that he went to her computer and checked that he was allowed to turn it off then did so.

'Web design too?' Gabe remarked. 'You can come to Broken Bridle and I'll give you a job.'

'I don't want an office job. I did it for longer than I ever wanted to. If running Pure Pleasures comes at the price of hard work, I'm willing to grab that deal.'

'OK, you're passionate about what you do, I get that.' Gabe smiled then sat on her desk edge. 'I came by to say I'm going out with my family tomorrow. I'm going to the stables to spend time with Ruth discussing her skittish rescued horse, but I'll come around in the afternoon to help you. Nancy's coming by to help at the store and your friend from the local farm, Sheila, says she'll drop by in the morning.'

As Jess ate her delicious food she realised that she was hungry; ravenous in fact. She tried not to wolf it down.

'Taken over as my PA now too?'

'No, just letting you know I listened to what you told me when we met. Josh and Ruth deserve their chances to make it work and I need to focus attention on things I can control. I'm wiping the slate clean and building bridges.'

Jess stared at him and widened her eyes. 'Wow. That's what I'd call an epiphany the size of an elephant for a guy who came here with a volcanic chip on his Stetson.'

Gabe faked a gun-slinger scowl. 'You sizing for a fight?'

Jess laughed. 'I'm the walking wounded, remember? I wouldn't stand a chance.'

'Don't underestimate yourself,' Gabe answered. His voice was a deep enticement that made her believe he meant it.

Jess cleared her throat. 'I'm pleased you're spending time with Ruth and Josh. You don't need to worry about me — just enjoy your well earned vacation and spend it with your family.'

Gabe leaned forward. 'In a round-about way that was a thank you . . . for helping me think things through. But the main reason I'm telling you is if I can wake up so can you. Jess, you need more permanent help.'

'Here we go again,' she muttered but Gabe slid a piece of paper into her hand. It bore a handwritten phone number.

'I met someone today. An Australian guy called Ray who's working a burger van at the stop-off scenic spot on the high road. We got chatting when I went to collect your prescription. He's a trained chef and in an ideal world he'd like somewhere to invest in someday. He plans on staying around.'

Jess stared. 'A chef running a burger bar? For the Flask?'

'The guy's talent is wasted. Just a tip off. His Tex-Mex Burger was fabulous.' Gabe grinned and waggled his brows.

Maybe it was fate. But was fate's major coup bringing her Ray, or bringing her Gabe Garrett?

Another chef would mean no more double shifts and if the guy was as good as Gabe thought . . .

Her grudging unwillingness and fear of criticism were morphing into quiet accepting agreement. Jess went into her lower desk drawer and retrieved her vintage tin box.

'Something for you in return.'

Gabe neared, so close she could feel his warmth. Hear his breathing. He let out a slow mmmn noise at the delicious aroma from the tin.

'Millionaire's shortbread. Chocolate and caramel on rich buttery shortcake. Take some, it's homemade. I made it a few days ago for tomorrow's coffee morning at the village hall.'

Gabe drew out one melting slab of decadence as Jess stowed away the chef details safely in her notebook.

'Poisoned. Is this how it's going to be? You lure me into a false sense of security then feed me poisoned edible delights?'

Jess burst out laughing.

Seconds later Gabe winked. 'You are good, aren't ya? My tastebuds will take the risk — what a way to go.'

★ ★ ★

Gabe enjoyed his shortbread.

And she'd enjoyed watching his enjoyment and hearing his jokes as he ate every sugary, melt-in-the-mouth scrap.

He'd actually begged her for a second piece.

She wasn't sure if he'd only done it to amuse her or if he really had a tooth that sweet.

Then he put his palm on Jess's elbow to make her rise and shepherded her out of her office. 'Time to head in. No more work. I'll see you safely inside, ma'am.'

As she locked up and he left her at the cottage door, she watched him as he chewed on his last pilfered slice of chocolate tray bake and walked away.

He wasn't at all the bad guy she'd pegged him as.

He was decent. Kind. Thoughtful.

Hard-working. Pragmatic. Intelligent. Caring.

Would he be heading in to bed? Or for a long herbal soak?

Do not spoil things with crazy fantasies. He'll be gone right after the wedding. He has a life all of his own thousands of miles from here.

Jess gulped. 'Sleep tight, Garrett. And thank you for helping. It's been mighty kind,' she whispered.

★   ★   ★

'Don't you envy them being so in love?' Nancy probed, the loch wind whirling her curls around. Gabe knew his sister was ever the romantic. She'd find love herself one day soon — he hoped it would be as soon as she wished it.

'One day I want that; to know I've found my place. My soulmate,' Nancy concluded as she watched her brother, Josh, and his soon-to-be bride.

Her sigh was the stuff of epic films and big doorstop romance novels. Gabe stood against the boat's railing and watched Ruth and Josh hug again as they sat aboard the small boat. He felt detached and distant. Had he really come to terms with losing Josh for good?

They'd gone for a visit to Dinnoch Monastery via tour boat. He'd taken Jess's lead and invited Josh and Ruth out. Happily they'd shelved most work commitments in the weeks leading up to the wedding and were equally keen for a Garrett family reunion so an impromptu monastery visit had been agreed.

Gabe didn't answer Nancy and took out his camera, taking snaps for posterity as a cover instead of making conversation.

And then it struck him — soon this would be all he'd have. A memory; snapshots.

Is this what the Garrett's future held? Snatched vacation glimpses and emailed images as the years sprinted through the circle of life. That thought darkened his heart.

Jess's voice echoed in the tunnel of his thoughts. *Families stick together through thick and thin.*

Suddenly all the good bridges he'd built up here — acceptance of his brother's wishes, positivity about the future — came crashing down in a messy, ugly, heap of broken ideals. Who was he kidding? He'd go back to Texas and they'd drift. How else could they hope to keep their links alive across the miles?

'Bet you're glad you came,' Nancy concluded. 'She's clearly so right for him.'

Gabe nodded. Nancy was right, Ruth was lovely. It was the wrench and distance he couldn't get past.

He was indeed losing his only brother.

There was nothing that could patch Texas and Scotland and pull them closer together on the map. Nothing.

'If Josh can make a hard choice, so can you. You deserve all the good things you want for yourself. You'll find someone soon,' said Nancy who then walked over to sit beside Josh and Ruth. Josh turned and met his gaze.

Did Nancy really think he envied Josh his luck?

It wasn't jealousy that had started this. Nor regrets about his ex who'd burned him. Marie, who'd promised her heart and proved herself ultimately fickle.

He'd never envied Josh finding Ruth. He'd envied him walking in the first place.

How could a man who was a billionaire twice over envy someone anything? Thanks to an oil dynasty inheritance from his godfather Joel, Gabe Garrett — and Josh and Nancy too — would never want for money again. They kept their fortunes secret. Why shout about something that wouldn't change your life or your lifestyle? They'd never be oil magnates; just the beneficiaries of one of the biggest oilfields in Dallas. Cowboys without a clue what to do with all the dollar bills in their bank accounts. Except philanthropy and valuable charity work. Their Momma had bred them to have a strong conscience.

Sure Gabe ran the ranch — but if he so chose he could never work again. That wouldn't happen though. The Garretts may be billionaires on paper but they'd always be a Texan ranching family at heart. It's what they'd always done.

Only now Josh had broken away.

'You feeling sea-sick, Gabe?' Josh asked. 'Lookin' weird.'

'I'm a ranch boy. Not a sea scout. I'll be fine in a minute. When I'm back on dry land.'

But it was nothing to do with the swell of the waves. It was Nancy crystallising that he'd stopped expecting good things and figured he was immune. He had the money, and he did plenty with it, but in his personal life he'd closed down the opportunities for good.

Was he closed and blinkered?

Was he blaming Josh when the one holding him back most was himself?

Gabe looked across the water — and straight at The Crofter's Flask which sat stout and white in the harbour like a beacon. His thoughts went straight to Jess. He'd love to capture this view on canvas for her.

And why had that crazy, stray thought popped inexplicably into his head?

He'd brought his sketch pad and kit with him figuring it would help pass the time. He wasn't prepared for how beautiful Scotland was, how the light was pure magic and the views inspirational. Painting was Gabe's secret pleasure but ranch work didn't allow for detours to art school.

The biggest irony was that he now funded several art school bursaries in his godfather's name. And a care home and several charitable trusts in his mother's. Yet he'd never let himself dream of doing what he'd most love to do at heart — letting himself live.

These days he dabbled with art. More often than not he avoided even letting himself tinker with that pleasure because he'd never be as good as he wanted. He didn't have the space in his life to pursue it.

He had a ranch to run. A billionaire's bank account to shoulder. This unassuming Texan cowboy only took busmen's holidays. Work and obligation were his mantras. The money did good for a lot of people.

But it hadn't changed him, not one bit.

6

Gabe Garrett had been at Rowan Croft for just less than a week and in that time he'd been more help than Jess could've bargained for. He'd moved her storeroom around, he'd worked on adding the huge piles of gravel to the parking lot outside Pure Pleasures to create extra parking spaces, a job she'd been meaning to do for months.

She'd figured it would be a job that would take a week. He'd achieved it in a day.

He'd arranged for Ray from the burger van to drop by and amazingly he and Jess had clicked really quickly. She'd given him an impromptu interview that went well, with a promise of a probationary trial at The Flask — he was due to start on Monday.

After fixing up her staffing crisis, Gabe had fixed gaps in the perimeter fence and had worked on Rowan Croft's wild but unkempt garden. He'd fixed new shutters and emptied gutters. He'd cut logs and painted the outhouse. He'd claimed he missed his usual ranch-work.

Somehow she couldn't help thinking that he was in league with Josh and Ruth to intervene.

At one time this would have riled her. Right now she could only feel grateful. He'd just got on and done the jobs without fuss. Every glimpse of him, working like a Trojan, had her heart skipping and twisting in her chest; her blood flowing fast and free in her veins.

And she wasn't the only one.

Suddenly her car lot had double the custom — mostly female.

Women came to the store more than usual, choosing to linger and chat to Gabe during visits. Sometimes they visited twice. Gabe Garrett it seemed, tended to cause a case of amnesia that involved forgetting half of what you'd come to purchase in the first place.

Women liked him.

With muscles like those it was scant wonder and it made Jess grin. Especially now she was more able and didn't have the strappings or bandages to hamper her checking up on him.

'You OK for provisions at the cottage?' Jess asked. The swelling had eased and though she was slower and wasn't yet able to carry a tray, she carried out a single glass of homemade lemonade to quench the cowboy's work-induced thirst.

The plate beside the glass was laden with caramel shortbread.

She'd heard it said on the grapevine that despite the fact Gabe had taken her tin of shortbread to the village hall sale — he'd also purchased and left with half of it too. So she'd had to make more, naturally.

Jess usually kept the holiday cottage clean and changed linens herself. But half her attention today had been on a phone call with her accountant. He'd been telling her about progress in their attempts to pursue venture capital for Pure Pleasures — a cash injection would really help her invest more in the business to take it to the next level.

'The cottage is perfect,' Gabe answered, welcoming her glass of juice and drinking half of it in a oner. 'As are the attentive refreshments. You've got your colour back, Jess, and it suits you.' He smiled.

She noted the beads of perspiration on his top lip; the tanned shoulders in a work vest that outlined a manual labourer's honed body. It made her feel like a smitten schoolgirl.

'Just looking after your welfare. Ruth told me she really enjoyed the family day out to the monastery. She's invited us to go and have supper with them at her place tonight.'

Gabe drank down the rest of the lemonade in one gulp.

He grinned at her. 'I'll come for dinner and drive us both there on one condition. Stop feeding me chocolate shortbread. I feel like you've discovered my weakness.'

'I'll think about it, Garrett,' Jess answered. 'I like having a weapon to use to make you obey my rules.'

* ★ ★

When Ben Logan stopped by for the second time that day, Jess figured it wasn't just her health he was interested in.

His jeep pulled up in the car lot and she watched him jump out. Trim and muscular through a regular windsurfing habit, she guessed Ben was quite a catch — just not the man for her.

At the nub of things, she sometimes found his conversation to be a little too self oriented. This may seem a small wrinkle in an otherwise smooth package, but she guessed there was just no spark there to tempt her.

'Hi Jess. You're looking great,' enthused Ben, heaping on the charm.

Jess looked up from her pursuit of

packing up boxes of fragrant soaps in purple tissue paper for an internet order. 'Thanks for dropping by. How can I help?'

Ben smiled. 'A favour. Tonight. I'd like to take you out.' The proof of the pudding of his continued interest.

Fortunately she had a good excuse.

'Sorry, Ben. It's too short notice. I've already agreed to go to Ruth and Josh's place for a barbecue. But thanks for the offer.' She really hoped he wouldn't push it and try to rearrange for another night. She'd honestly felt like she'd got off the hook when Ben had stopped his dating pursuit of her before.

'That's great. I need to speak to Josh and he won't mind me tagging along. I'll call them to make sure it's OK.'

Jess hesitated to answer. For one, her own opinion on the topic was that to push yourself into a private dinner date was not only rude but thoughtless. For two, she was wary about a night ahead with Ben Logan and Gabe Garrett — two primed Spartan warriors ready to draw blood over honour and ego. Not good.

'Um . . . would you like me to call and arrange it?' Jess swiftly offered, thinking perhaps if she had a chance to speak to Ruth they might hatch a get-out clause between them.

'No. Don't go to any trouble. I'll see you there. I want to talk to you about something. A business matter. We'll talk later. Though I would still like to take you out to dinner another time. Seeing you the other night got to me more than I imagined — I realised how much you still mean to me, Jess.'

His blue eyes nailed her. He was slightly closer than she'd like. For a doctor his people skills could do with some work.

'I'm really not sure, Ben. You know I talked about needing space before. Nothing's changed.'

'Just dinner, Jess. I'm not talking a wedding at Invergarry Castle.'

Jess felt foolish as if she'd been

inferring Ben was more into her than he was. But she also felt testy at him for talking to her like a child. And an idiot. For someone interested in getting her on side he wasn't doing a very good job.

He must've sensed her reticence. 'It's only dinner. Nothing heavy — just you and me and some gentle chat and catch up time. It's good to get out and catch up with old friends after all. Let's talk tonight.' Ben already had his keys back out of his pocket and was throwing them from hand to hand impatiently.

Jess smiled. Was she too closed off . . . too suspicious?

'Sure,' she ventured. 'As long as it's a date between friends?'

'Sure, whatever makes you say yes.'

When Ben left it took a good five minutes for his overly strong cologne to fade. It irritated her nostrils in a way Gabe's earthy natural cedarwood scent never did.

And she felt guilty — just recognising it.

'Hey — these are good. Not just good. Amazing!' said Jess, taking in the scene before her.

Gabe had been sitting by the loch in a deck-chair. She'd wondered if he was bird-spotting or sleeping in the sun and had gone to check, only to find that he was sitting with a small easel propped open, brushes and paint palette in hand and a watercolour in progress coming to life before him.

The likeness was terrific. His touches were deft and delicate and surprising for a man so rugged and strong.

When it came to artwork he had a most excellent eye and a finely tuned touch.

'You didn't tell me you paint?'

Gabe looked embarrassed and it made her like him all the more. 'Don't be shy,' she encouraged. 'You really are good.'

'You're not going to say I'm awful to my face, now are you?' Gabe refuted, stopping his work.

'Don't stop. Can I look?' Jess asked.

Gabe handed her the sketchbook at his feet. There were lots of paintings and sketches. People, places, views. And already a smattering of Scottish scenes she recognised.

'You've painted the pub.'

'Sorry, should I have asked permission?'

'Don't be daft. It's fabulous. Don't suppose I could buy it. I'd love to frame it and hang it in there for regulars to admire.'

Gabe shrugged. 'Who'd want to look at that.'

Jess put her hands on her hips.

His attitude was starting to get her down and he needed telling straight.

'Surely you've been trained at art school. Nobody just paints like that without work and practice and tuition.'

'Never had a stroke of advice — other than stop. Ranchers don't regularly prance around with brushes in

139

their hand making pretty paintings for a lady's parlour.'

'Maybe they would if they had your talent.'

'Look. Can we change the subject?' Gabe checked his watch. 'We'd better go change if we're going to make it to Josh's on time. I need to shower first.'

'But you haven't finished your painting,' Jess protested.

'It's only a doodle.'

'Can I borrow your pad? I won't spoil any of the pictures. I just really like that view of the loch. I'd love a copy for the store.'

'Have it,' said Gabe packing up his bits noisily and shoving everything into a large satchel like a guilty secret. His expression looked closed and wary.

'But you haven't signed them yet.'

He shrugged.

Jess folded the sketchpad shut and kept quiet on Gabe's surly and sceptical reaction. It bothered her that he was so defensive and closed. He did have talent and skill no matter what he said.

She secretly vowed to make sure those paintings would be hung some place people would see them. In frames and behind glass like they deserved. Even if they were unloved. And unsigned.

★ ★ ★

'So,' Gabe said as he started up his hire car's engine and smiled when it purred and he began to drive out of the Pure Pleasures parking area. 'You're not working. This is progress; a rare view of Jess Gilmour socialising. I'm very impressed. Ten out of ten,' Gabe said and looked pleased.

'Don't talk to me like I'm back at school and you're the teacher everybody loves to hate.'

He nodded to her arm. 'Your sling is off and your ankle looks good in those sandals. In fact, I was about to say you're looking lovely tonight . . . if that isn't too personal an observation.'

Secretly she relished the compliments.

And the smell of his shower-fresh scent and his still-damp hair. She particularly enjoyed the fact that even though he'd showered he'd missed a couple of paint smudges on his hands. It proved to her he was a painter; it was ingrained.

Bottom line, Gabe scrubbed up very well.

Jess looked down at her own espadrille sandals as a cover instead of looking at Gabe Garrett more than she should be.

She kept her hands in her lap; hoped they weren't shaking under his scrutiny. She'd actually worn a dress. OK, it was just a casual cotton sunflower yellow sundress worn with a white lacey cotton shrug, but getting Jess out of her favourite baseball boots and jeans was something — plus there was a gentle touch of lipgloss and blush.

She figured tonight was a special occasion. This was the first 'official introduction dinner' between brides-maid and best man. Or it would've been had a certain doctor not gone and muscled in on arrangements.

What was getting into her?

One thing was for sure, her glammed up appearance certainly wasn't for Ben Logan.

Ruth had called her earlier and told her that he'd had the cheek to claim to need to see Josh urgently and he'd invited himself without apology. She'd been less than impressed; fuming fit to burst, had been her exact words.

So if the dress wasn't for Ben, who was it for?

A sexy neighbourhood cowboy to impress? Certainly not.

A man who hitched her pulse and made her remember she was female . . . one who'd held her in his strong, bold embrace more than once and made palpitations and flutters of attraction spiral within?

No. She was sensible. Rational. Careful, prudent.

And just because the bridesmaid and the best man got together in rom coms and books didn't mean that was on the cards here.

Jess sighed and fixed her gaze on the road ahead. This wasn't good. She wasn't usually so upended by things. She should've worn her favourite combat shorts and khaki top. And acted prim and professional at all times, keeping Gabe and Ben both at bay.

Only Ben was a way more easier proposition to manage than Gabe was. She always managed to say no to him.

She wished she hadn't noticed how good Gabe looked in a pale aqua polo shirt tonight. It was worn over new dark denim board shorts; with no socks and deck shoes. She definitely shouldn't notice his athletic frame and strong bronzed legs.

'So. Do you intend to show me your prowess as the barbecue king, tonight?' Jess asked, striving for serious and interesting.

Gabe grinned. 'Damn. How did you guess?'

Jess shook her head. 'Call it a hunch. Do you always have to be so competitive? Are all cowboys trained in it at school? Does it come as a complimentary bonus with your first lasso?'

Gabe laughed. 'Cowboy code again darlin'. Miss Jessica — surely you should be gettin' the hang of the ways of the west by now. We're born to show we're the better man.'

She had to laugh at that. 'I'm getting used to you. Still contrary, just like your sister says.'

He scoffed slightly. 'Oh, yep. You don't like challenging men. You prefer boring, sensible doctor types like Jealous Guy Desk Bore Logan. He doesn't like me. He breathes fire when I get too close which kinda makes me want to do it all the more. He almost ran me over in the village the other day. Accidentally on purpose of course.'

'You'll just have to get your shotgun and your spurs out to show him who's top dog. Perhaps you shouldn't succumb to silly schoolboy games, Gabe Garrett,' teased Jess.

Jess stared at Gabe as they swiftly rounded the bend in the lane and she pointed out the entrance way to Ruth's stables — Dinnoch Whins Equestrian Centre — sitting behind a vast screen of rhododendron bushes and lush foliage. It was a lovely, sunny, balmy night; perfect al fresco evening dinner weather. The Gods had seen fit to bless then with good fortune.

'You really have time for a guy with a stethoscope and a God complex?' Gabe probed. 'I thought you had good taste. Isn't he a little boring for a woman like you?'

'Don't be so hard on him. He isn't that bad. And he's not boring. Actually . . . he is boring. But don't ever tell him I said so. And don't think that makes me condone your competitive ways.'

Smiling to himself Gabe pulled up in the parking spaces by Ruth's main house. Only the smile was about to fade fast.

'Lover boy at twelve o'clock. The night's just taken a downward turn,' said Gabe. 'Your Doctor Logan is crashing the party. Over there on the terrace deck.'

Jess hadn't dared mentioned Ben's earlier visit. She'd sensed Gabe might cancel the whole thing.

As if on cue Ben Logan raised his brimming glass in greeting.

Gabe didn't smile. His jaw looked firm and his lips were in a tight line.

'I'll go fire up some steaks and take my aggression out on the barbecue,' said Gabe. 'If there's smoke and flames later, you know my temper's gone incendiary.'

His lack of scruples about showing his dislike was refreshingly funny.

When Jess turned to get out of the car Gabe stopped her, his hand warm and large on her elbow. It tingled, and made her lightly gasp.

'Shame to waste a dress the colour of

ripe corn on a May morning that looks so good the horses would swoon, on a guy like that,' he said softly. 'You deserve so much better. Cut him loose and try fun with me instead. I'll be making the food taste great. And putting rat-poison in his burger.'

Jess had to laugh, then stifle her giggles as Ruth came out of the house to meet them, followed by Josh.

'Hey. You're here. Salad's done and the barbecue is starting up nicely. How about a drink on the terrace? Your very own doctor is here to make sure you're behaving yourself . . . I didn't realise you needed such critical medical attention.' Ruth raised her brows in silent heavy meaning.

Gabe surprised them all when he hooted with faked laughter when Ben looked over. Gabe smiled straight at Jess on purpose and it made her pulse leap and hitch when his eyes blatantly devoured her all on their own.

'Leave my landlady alone. I'm here only as personal protection for those legs in that dress. He steps outta line, it'll be Alamo Round Two.'

But as Ben came to greet her, further banter with the cowboy would have to keep for later.

★　★　★

Jess sat on the wall outside Ruth's stables and took the apple Ruth threw her to snack on.

'We'll spoil dinner,' Jess challenged.

'Don't sweat it — it'll take a while. Josh and Gabe are working on the barbecue. You know how men get when roasting meat — they go all primal when they don an apron and get full access to barbecue tongs. I'm glad to see you looking well again.'

'Thank you, I feel better. Where's Nancy tonight?' Jess enquired.

'Hot date!' Ruth winked. 'Ryan Duncan — he owns the new Seafood Bistro at Dinnoch Point — she's captured his interest.'

'Fraternising with the competition?

Actually Nancy's been a miracle worker — she's brilliant with my customers in the store. She loves the work there too!'

'And what about Gabe?'

'What about him?'

Ruth faked a sigh. 'I didn't realise how lovely Gabe would be, I had him pegged as a trouble-maker and I was wrong,' Ruth conceded. 'Just goes to show what prejudice does. I honestly never thought he'd come here and make such an effort. Put his grumbles aside. So what do you think?'

Jess knew some of the truths behind Gabe's attitude.

He was trying hard — that didn't mean he was finding it easy.

But he had a loyal cowboy code that meant he ranked his family highly — even if it was painful for him in the process.

Jess decided that was surely Gabe's private business.

'Maybe he's realised he's been too harsh in his judgements,' Jess concluded and crunched her apple. 'He's still a bossy boots who likes his own way.'

'He's my future brother-in-law. I'm going to be a Garrett. You like him, don't you?'

Jess raised her eyes. 'He seems to think he has a right to run my business — but I'm guessing he feels protective after I had that dramatic fainting turn. I have to admit, he's been a big help. And he's the head of the Garrett family now. I think he's just found it hard finding his views coming last.'

Ruth winked slowly. 'And he's built with an exceptional masculine chassis too?'

'Can't say I've noticed,' Jess lied.

'No kidding. When Invergarry's women are flocking to your store for a close-up view? How on earth can you stand watching that man's muscles without drooling? It's all over the village that Jess Gilmour has employed a male model to work outside her store as an advertisement.'

'I wouldn't stoop so low,' said Jess and they both laughed.

Jess considered covering her feelings about Gabe with a lie. In the end she decided there was little point when already half the women in Invergarry were aflame with talk of Gabe Garrett's assets and visiting her soap store because of him. He was very good for her business. And easy on the eye.

'It's enough to drive a nun crazy,' Jess said then burst into laughter. Ruth laughed so much she nearly toppled over the wall.

'So you've had Turnaround Central on your new brother-in-law,' Jess stated.

'I think I'm not the only one who should reconsider her principles and be more open to change,' Ruth conceded.

'Meaning?'

'Gabe. There's clearly sparks between you. All he thinks about is helping you out and making sure you're considering your needs. He told us you've helped him get down off his high horse.'

'He's being modest.'

'And you've worn a widow's cloak way too long. Why not enjoy some attention for a change . . . you can't hide from romance forever, Jess.'

'Ben doesn't like him,' said Jess.

'And Ben is Mr Boring. You know you'd never in a million years have settled down with him. He's just not your type.'

'What is my type?'

'Someone who knows himself,' Ruth replied.

'Like Dan did?'

'No. Not at all.' Ruth looked solemn. 'You need someone who can stand up to you on your own terms, Jess Gilmour. I think Gabe Garrett is the closest you've come to finding that.'

'I think pre-wedding vibes are turning you soppy,' Jess replied. 'When I need a man, I'll get one.'

'Make sure you do. There's nothing I'd like more for you.'

Jess took a last bite from her apple before feeding the remains to Ruth's horse, Ginger. It vanished in one almighty crunched bite and Ginger eyed her speculatively. Ruth's words were still difficult for Jess to swallow.

'Let's go walk around the paddock,' she said, trying to change the conversation. 'Apparently I need to give my ankle gentle exercise. Plus I need to keep away from Ben.'

Even she knew she was running scared.

Not just from Ben — from her attraction to Gabe.

Jess hadn't admitted to anyone that she'd already joined Team Garrett by her own choice. There was only one man who'd turned her head and he wore a Stetson not a stethoscope.

*   *   *

With a stomach full of delicious barbecue fare that had included the finest local steaks, burgers and chargrilled veggies, plus Ruth's signature salads galore, Gabe and Jess bid farewell to her friends just before midnight.

They waved back at the happy

couple. Ben had gone an hour earlier, thankfully realising five was a crowd.

'Of course you realise Josh is going to move out just before the wedding as a nod to tradition,' Jess remarked.

'Of course. Tradition's important. Josh is an old- fashioned, well brought up guy . . . ' Gabe stared at the road ahead.

'I'm guessing you both are.'

'Naturally. Best get you home before you turn into a pumpkin,' said Gabe.

'You say the most charming things, Mr Garrett.'

He revisited his words. 'We had a good time tonight, didn't we? Don't think Ben will be bothering you again, either. I let it slip that you've got your beady eye on the gamekeeper.'

'Archie Williams. He's fifty-five in three weeks time!'

'Don't backtrack Gilmour. We did a great job and threw him off the scent.'

'And you just called me a pumpkin. And now you're spreading scurrilous rumours.'

He stared at her for some moments, flicking a tongue out to moisten his lips. 'You've plenty of Cinderella potential, Jess Gilmour. Don't doubt it because you do. You looked amazing tonight. I'll be a proud best man the day I stand up in church beside you as Ruth's bridesmaid.'

Jess smiled. 'Why thank you. That's very gallant. As best men go you're growing on me too.'

They drove for some way in silence. Devoid of street lights, the long tree-lined avenue leading to Pure Pleasures seemed extra dark and there was no other traffic on the road. It felt like they were the only humans on the planet — and how would Jess Gilmour feel if Gabe was the last man on earth and she was the last woman?

A tiny treacherous part of her got instantly excited and belied her true feelings. Damn.

'I mean it when I compliment you, Jess. I don't flatter women lightly. It's not my style.'

'Thanks Gabe. But since you're a guy who thinks horses are gorgeous, I'll take it with a pinch of salt.'

His eyes were serious, his voice was rusty. He held her firmly in his gaze and reached out to take her hand. 'Don't deflect me. You really don't realise what a true sparkling gem you are.' He fixed her with a chastening glance.

'Oh, no!' Jess's expression changed in an instant, but not because of the words he'd spoken.

Gabe followed her horrified gaze towards Rowan Croft. The door was wide open. The garden gate too.

She went to get out of the car but Gabe's firm hand stopped her. 'Hold off a minute — let me see first, won't you?'

Jess nodded, her breath coming fast. Her heart raced, she felt a little dizzy but it was just shock. In all the years she'd lived here she'd never felt scared or alone or odd about the tiny isolated corner she called home. Suddenly she felt like it had been violated.

'A burglar? But this is no crime hotspot . . .'

'Shh!' Gabe put his finger to her mouth. Her lips buzzed with the contact of his warm skin. 'Relax, OK,' he said on a whisper.

He strode from the car.

Jess got out behind him.

'I meant for you to wait,' he whispered.

'It's my property. I'm coming with you.'

Her eyes must've told of her panic because he squeezed her hand before leading her towards the cottage.

And that's when they saw the glass. The window had been broken and a brick lay in the sink of Rowan Croft's kitchen.

Jess gasped and tried to calm herself down.

Gabe Garrett quickly confirmed her suspicions with a dark look and tight words. 'If I'm not mistaken that's definitely not the work of squirrels with a grudge. And I've never seen a prairie dog big enough to throw a brick.'

'We don't have prairie dogs in Scotland, Gabe.'

'Then I think we should keep calm. But we should also call the police,' Gabe told her firmly.

7

Jess felt somewhat self conscious when she awaited Gabe's arrival for breakfast next morning. She wasn't wearing her usual relaxed, casual denim gear — today she had an important meeting at ten. One lined up with an interested venture capitalist by her accountant.

She was quietly crossing her fingers — and everything else — that it would go well. After last night's shock, she needed some good news.

The police had inspected the damaged window but doubted a culprit would be tracked down. At least nothing else was damaged or touched.

Pure Pleasures really could do with a business boost right now too — she needed to expand and allow it to grow to fulfil its potential but that needed cashflow reserves she just didn't have. Not now anyway.

'Mornin' ma'am,' said Gabe then flashed her attire a meaningful look. Her best suit was behind her apron for protection but it wasn't hidden. He nodded his approval. 'Going somewhere special?'

'A meeting with a company who run a chain of tourist shops around the highlands. They have stores all over — Pitlochry, Glencoe, Inverness. Having their support for Pure Pleasures would be a big boost. It would get Pure Pleasures much needed attention and backing.'

Gabe smiled. 'You'll do yourself proud.'

'I'm a little nervous,' Jess admitted.

'They'd be lucky to have you.'

Jess dished up Gabe's full Scottish breakfast, plated his toast and carried him his tray. 'Now sit and have your breakfast. You're making me even more nervous talking about it.'

'Yes ma'am. Not only a captain of industry but the best breakfast cook in the country.' He eyed the breakfast banquet before him. 'How lucky I am to have found you.'

'And now that you've overdosed me with compliments — what are your plans for today?' Jess asked deflecting all the attention away from her nerves and her plight.

'Actually I intend to paint by the loch and make the most of this fine day. I might not be a great master but there are some views I'd like to sit and try to capture. I'm rusty but sometimes I manage to make smudges in the right places on the paper.'

Jess said softly, 'Actually I have a confession on that score. The sketch of the inn. It's been framed and it's hanging up behind the bar. I wanted to show it off.'

Gabe shrugged and acted humble. 'I guess I'll just have to bear seein' it then. I just enjoy it. Beats chasing cattle and mending fences every moment of the day. Painting is my chillax time. Doesn't matter if what I produce isn't that worthy of hanging on a wall.'

'Good for you, but I think it's more than worthy. And I'm pleased to hear that Gabe Garrett sometimes takes time to stop and enjoy life too.'

'Might also go and talk to the local policeman. See what he's saying about last night's incident,' Gabe confided, his tone more serious and sombre.

'A glazier will be popping by later, he'll fix the window so it won't inconvenience you further,' Jess explained. 'Sheila from the farm is manning Pure Pleasures and she'll see to the glazier when he gets here. Hopefully it'll all be back to normal later.'

'You're not worrying about that are you?'

Jess shook her head.

She'd had little time to think about it and no real clues what to think. She had, in truth, pushed it firmly from her mind.

What was the point in jumping to lots of negative and upsetting conclusions about the brick through her guest cottage window when for all she knew it may just be prankster kids and some high jinx that had gone awry?

Right now she had enough on her plate without getting bogged down in wondering about things she couldn't help. Though deeper down she wasn't comfortable about any of it. Not now that her property had been damaged without explanation.

'The policeman didn't have much to go on,' Jess said on a shrug. 'No fingerprints. Nothing.'

'Actually I found a footprint,' said Gabe and Jess widened her eyes in surprise.

'When?'

'This morning; first light. A boot print — could be nothin'. But then again . . . ' said Gabe in a casual, easy way. 'I've put an old bucket around it to protect the evidence. And I've taken photographs. I figure I'll get PC Mackay to come back later and run his eye over what I've found. It's not much, but it's better than nothing. Try not to worry about it, Jess; it's all in hand. Try not to concern yourself unduly.'

He wasn't going to mention how unique the print was and what it pointed to. The fact it gave him a hunch about what had happened and who was at the root of it.

'Ranch boss knows best,' Jess said patting her hair into place in its neat chignon style, putting her keys and phone in her briefcase and re-checking her watch. 'OK if I go? I don't want to be late. I'm afraid I won't see you later — dashing around a lot today. And tonight is Ruth's hen night. A small, select gathering at the pub, or that's how it started. Somewhere along the line all the women in the region have come to be invited and are attending. In fancy dress too. So I may not see you until tomorrow, Gabe.'

'Go and enjoy yourself. Remember — they'd be lucky to have you; this company that you're going to meet. Be picky. You're in the driving seat — not them. Interviews are a two way thing.'

Jess nodded and Gabe threw her a

devastating smile. 'And last thing to remember . . . '

'What's that?' said Jess, her hand on the door knob. 'More orders from the ranch boss?'

He grinned and his smile was one hundred watt knock out. 'I like what you're wearing. The smart look suits you. But I liked you most of all last night in that dress. Hope I'll be taking you out to dinner in it to celebrate a bright new deal very soon. Knock 'em dead, Miss Jessica.'

She nodded and left, blushing at his endearments as she walked to her van. The look in his eyes when he'd given those compliments had made something inside her tummy tremble and melt.

Jess wholly intended to do the very best she could. Not just for herself — for Gabe Garrett too.

* * *

Gabe wasn't telling Jess the full truth though he had good reason. For now he didn't want to worry her or get her hopes up unduly.

Personally he was quietly assured that they'd get to the bottom of the window-smashing mystery. He might be jumping the Texan cowboy's gun but he already figured he knew who was to blame.

It wasn't just because the man didn't like him. And Gabe liked Ben Logan even less. There was no love lost.

Especially now Gabe suspected he'd come over here and caused damage to Jess's property just to give a silent back-off message. To underline his territory and his stake.

Only thing was Gabe was a rancher. Born and bred. He had instincts when it came to trouble; rustlers and mysteries that reeked of foul play.

Ben Logan was the window breaking prankster, of that he was certain.

He'd come here on foot and snagged his fancy pants on the barbed fence by Jess's broken wall. He'd parked his jeep in the loch's overflow car park

— Gabe had found wide car tracks that he'd bet would match the doctor's tyres. He'd even taken the trouble to put on a pair of Jess's over-sized plastic beach sandals — discarded on her cottage porch — to create false tracks. But in doing so he'd put fingerprints all over the shiny, foam plastic shoes. Would that be enough?

They were shoes that were Jess's. Dr Logan could easily have retrieved them from the basket on her porch. They were also too small and had caused a print that showed a man's heel overhanging the uniquely printed sole. Ranch boys noticed such things; call it a hang up from playing trapper games in the wild in his youth.

Gabe doubted he'd be charged for such a minor offence though the incriminating evidence — the beach shoe prints and the snagged fabric from his trousers — gave him the upper hand. It was all Gabe wanted to put the sinister doctor well and truly back in his place.

Jess didn't need to know.

Gabe had it all firmly in hand and felt easier for his superior knowledge — he'd deal with Ben Logan in good time.

* * *

Jess breathed deep and tried to play light-hearted. A very short denim skirt, cowboy boots, plaid shirt tied at the waist and a pink cowgirl hat adorned with pink fur edging were hardly a come hither combo.

Ruth's hen night theme of choice was Cowgirls Go Wild, in honour of the Garretts' roots. She figured she'd just have to smile and get into the spirit.

It didn't help her mood any that the meeting with the investor had been a total waste of time and effort. The chain hadn't been as serious as she'd hoped. Plus the fit of their business wasn't quite right; the chain in question wasn't as high-end quality focused. It became patently apparent the manager of Highland Crafts and Souvenirs Inc liked to talk his own business up and had more bluff than real credentials to recommend him.

Secretly she'd got her hopes up about finding fresh investment and now she felt like a failure.

Jess sighed. Even her make-up verged on drag after she'd been pinned to the chair by Gabe's sister then forced to relent to glittery showgirl eyes.

She looked like an extra from some am-dram production of *Oklahoma*!

'You look good enough to eat,' said Nancy slipping her long glossy purple nails around Jess's arm. 'Stop worryin' and go with the flow, Jess.'

Easy to say when you hadn't just had your business dreams and confidence dashed.

Somehow Jess wasn't convinced even if she was impressed by Nancy's vibrant manicure. Like her cowboy brother, Nancy was forcing her places she wasn't ready to go and making her feel lacking in the fun stakes, too.

'It's a bachelorette party — cling on for the ride and smile,' Nancy ordered.

Jess shook her head.

'You look stunning. I on the other hand look like a twenty-eight-year old playing dress up — this isn't a good look for me.'

'It's just for kicks and to make Ruth smile. Where's the harm, honey?'

'That I'll be up 'til dawn removing the make-up with a pan scrubber. I'm worried my real eyelashes will come off with the false ones.'

They walked over the cobblestone path to The Crofter's Flask. 'I'll book you in for a facial. Or glue them back on myself. You should come to Tall Trees Creek — a walk on the wild side, Texas style. Maybe you need a Texan vacation? Gabe mentioned you work way too hard.'

Jess Gilmour had enough on her plate to keep her occupied without far flung vacations. Secretly it bothered her to hear that Gabe had been discussing her, even though it was with his sister.

Tonight Nancy sported Dukes of Hazard hot pants and a strappy denim top worn with a leather waistcoat. Next to her Jess felt like she was Calamity Cowgirl.

Jess convinced herself it was the outfit that was messing with her mood. It was OK for Nancy who'd look sparkly in a sack. Plus one look at her brothers, you recognised the magical genes.

'Texas is a long way for business expenses,' Jess answered.

Nancy held her shoulders between her palms. 'You've arranged a fantastic night. I know it's not your kind of thing but you have to loosen up.'

She had been preoccupied with arrangements for tonight's party. Catering arrangements at the pub — plus Ray had just started and though he'd needed induction into the way things were run at the pub, he'd begun well.

If only the hired-in-specially Bucking

Bronco machine installed at the pub as the centrepiece for festivities had been as glitch-free as Ray had been. It had experienced a few technical difficulties — either going very slow or super fast. As bridesmaid and organiser of the party and pub owner combined, the buck always rested with Jess — even if she had absolutely zilch experience of how to fix glitches with machinery that faked a rodeo horse.

As owner of the pub, all things reflected on Jess. So bachelorette fun and fancy dress garb was out of her comfort zone. Especially when it involved a memory lane of matrimony.

Even though, the pub was bedecked with a 'Ruth's Wild West Party' banner over its open door and inside country and western style rock music pulsed like tom toms.

Nancy threw her arms in the air as she danced ahead to whoops of encouragement from the others. All around them women wore cowgirl hats and were grinning from ear to ear

— some even had water pistols in holsters.

In spite of herself Jess laughed out loud. Marriage hadn't worked out for her, but that didn't mean it would be that way for Ruth and Josh.

'Let's get the party started!' Jess commanded.

She really didn't want to be here. But sometimes you just had to pretend.

★   ★   ★

Cowboys were supposed to be serious, sombre souls.

So why had he agreed to Nancy's pestering and bribes to be the barman at Ruth's bridal fun night?

'Maybe this wasn't such a good idea,' Gabe said inwardly, watching as another gaggle of fake cowboy hat bedecked females squeezed through the pub door and flocked on him all at once demanding spritzers and cocktails he hadn't even heard of. They were full of compliments, sure, but somehow he

174

now felt like a juicy, appetising mouse being sized up by giant female cats ready for their supper.

Gabe hoped hard that his little sister would get here soon to help him out with the cocktails. Two seconds later he saw her shimmy through the door and he motioned with his head for her to get behind the counter as quickly as she could.

If his ranch crew back home could see him now, he'd be a laughing stock. Mack would tease him for wearing a Stetson to serve drinks in. Jake would laugh his ass off and Murphy would have taken photographs so that the whole of Texas could enjoy his anguish.

Gabe clamped his jaw firm.

He should have refused and stayed clear of the shenanigans.

Gabe adjusted his chaps over his jeans as Nancy got to his side and began fast-draw drinks prep beside him.

'Thought you'd never get here, sis.'

'Don't worry. You're here as eye candy. Take the money and just smile and act dashing. And undo another button. You need to aim for hot honcho — not grouchy and embarrassed.'

Nancy's comment was like water on a flaming oil pan.

'Eye candy? I'm so embarrassed.'

'They've had so many cocktails they won't care. It's just a bit of light-hearted fun.'

Gabe saw his own nostrils flare in the mirror behind the bar. Nancy reached forward to snag at his western checked shirt. 'They want a hot barman, not choir boy. Buttons out.'

'How come the groom doesn't have to endure this humiliation?'

'Tradition. He can't. It's bad luck. So you're understudy. Can't have a Wild West Hen Night without a real life cowboy present to thrill the guests.'

Gabe threw her a blazing stare that threatened imminent murder. He grudgingly unhooked two buttons. A well honed chest peeped out just as the colour along Gabe's angular cheek-bones turned scarlet.

'Happy?'

'Delirious. Especially given how mad this is making you.'

Nancy's tongue was firmly in her cheek — a fact that only riled Gabe more.

Just then three women who'd been eyeing Gabe up like something on sale in a boutique window, seized their moment to strike by asking if later he'd do them the honour of a line dance.

Gabe had thought his humiliation couldn't get worse. It just had. He glared and his sister gave him a 'be nice' eye-roll.

'I'd be mighty obliged to show you the ropes,' he answered through gritted teeth.

'Loosen up, Gabriel. You only get one life,' Nancy told him softly. 'Jess is trying her best to make this a good night. We're all doing our bit for Ruth. Don't be cowardly and run at the first hurdle.'

His sister's words resonated. He'd always figured he was brave, so what was stopping him and why had the ranch become his raison d'etre by default? Why did he duck some issues and flee — like the future of Broken Bridle Ranch and how that figured with his long-term happiness?

The three women walked away, happy with their promises of a dance later. Gabe hand groomed his cropped dark hair and plopped his Stetson back on top. If he placed it low over his eyes he could just pretend this wasn't happening.

Gabe scowled. The strains of *Apache* by The Shadows began and Gabe could hear the sixty-odd female crowd whooping and laughing. Some were dancing and a DJ was starting to whip them up into a frenzy ready for the bronco machine.

Nancy whispered, 'You're doing this for Jess. I know how much you like her. Just think of it as a badge of honour. It's not often my billionaire cowboy big brother finds a woman good enough to fire his interest . . . '

How on earth had his little sister worked that one out?

'We're friends, Nancy.'

'If you say so, Gabriel. First friend I've ever seen you turn into Mr Attentive and Ultra Protective over.'

'She's up against it.'

'She's lovely. She deserves a knight in shining armour. Just noticing that your Texan charm act isn't as rusty as I'd thought.'

'You're seeing things.'

Nancy rattled her cocktail shaker and the look on her face told him she'd made her mind up already and didn't believe a word he said.

'Well, well, look who's just walked in,' Gabe said to no-one but himself.

Gabe saw Ben Logan standing by the pub door. He looked like a fish out of water. For one, he wasn't dressed in western party mode. For two, there weren't many men around this evening for obvious reasons.

What was with this guy and his tendency to turn up where he wasn't wanted?

Nancy shrugged, not realising the significance of the latest arrival to the party.

Gabe vowed to keep a steady, close watch on Dr Logan.

Especially when it came to Jess Gilmour. Call it a rattlesnake alert instinct but Gabe figured there was something afoot and he was determined to keep his enemy close.

* * *

'Hi Jess!' Ben came over and tried to grab her attention while Jess was handing out Texas flag cupcakes. In the middle of a hen-night, too. She was almost tempted to ask him who'd called a doctor.

She must've looked at him oddly because he said by way of explanation, 'Sorry to disturb you during the party. I was on my way home and I've been trying to track you down. I wondered if we could have a word. We didn't manage to talk to each other much at Josh and Ruth's place.'

'I didn't realise men were allowed tonight. Even doctors.'

Ben shrugged and gave her his best charmer's smile. 'I wanted to speak to you. I was worried about you. I went by Pure Pleasures today and they told me you had a window smashed last night. Nasty business.'

Jess was contrite and grateful for his patent concern. 'Yes, but it's nothing to worry about though. Thanks anyway.'

Ben's expression was grave. His grey eyes stayed on her face as he said, 'I worry about you being out there with nobody to protect you. It's not safe for a woman to be on her own at such an isolated spot.'

'I can look after myself. I'm a big girl. All these years and it's the first incident that's ever occurred. It's probably a kids' prank or something.' Jess felt like Annie Oakley when she pushed back her too big cowgirl hat. It now felt faintly ridiculous.

She felt like she should get out a shotgun as proof. Maybe if she had one she could try to use it on Ben to shoo him off once and for all.

'Look — can we go for a talk outside?' Ben said looking annoyed by the dancing females whooping all around them.

'It's not the best time.'

Jess tried to hide her sense of surprise and bubbling irritation that Ben Logan had come here tonight. It was after all a hen night. Men were sparse. The music was loud. This wasn't an ideal location for a quiet talk. Ben certainly knew how to pick his times.

The Good, The Bad and The Ugly roared from the speakers.

Some women were doing a conga around the bronco machine. The DJ had a lasso and was offering to give lessons. It couldn't be more bizarre if it tried.

Gabe Garrett was also watching her

from the bar area looking like the archetypal brooding gunslinger in a Western saloon.

He might be decanting glasses from the industrial dishwasher but his steady, wary gaze told her she had his attention. And so did Ben. Back off vibes bounced off the pair of them as they clocked each other and made no friendly greeting.

Jess inwardly groaned.

Gabe was wearing his Stetson and jeans and a skin tight white T-shirt. At some recent point he'd removed his shirt. The women were watching him and drooling into their drinks. With leather chaps and boots he was sexy cowboy defined.

Jess knew at heart she'd been trying to avoid watching him all night. He looked so good it was like being a dieter watching a large slice of cake that was totally off limits. One with lashings of fresh cream and gleaming, beckoning chocolate ganache.

Jess vowed to keep her calorie

counting head on while her Texan guest was in situ.

Gabe also had a crowd of hangers-on cooing over his every word around the end of the bar counter. She didn't want to spoil his popularity. They were keeping him occupied serving them drinks and he looked none too pleased about any of it. She was sure if he had a horse waiting outside he'd soon crack a whip and escape on it leaving a cloud of dust behind him.

Turning back to Ben, she stifled her irritation.

'Right, let's go, but I don't have long. I'm the organiser. We have a series of fun things planned for Ruth and I'm time-keeper. Can this be a quick chat?'

'Of course.' Ben's jaw flexed and he drew her close.

Gabe stared hard at them as she followed Ben out towards the pub's back garden terrace.

She hoped he wouldn't monopolise her for long or wasn't about to ask her out again. She was tired of his relentless misplaced pursuit.

So it took her by surprise completely when they got there and Ben turned her to face him then suddenly said, 'I'm worried about you being out there solo, Jess — so there's something I have to ask you. I've been considering it for some time. I'd like to make a proposal — a serious one. I'd like us to go into business together. I'm looking for an investment and I want to buy a share in Rowan Croft Holiday Lets.'

8

Gabe took a sip from his iced-water. He enjoyed a series of refreshing swallows after being in a heated, body-filled bar — a bar full of women offering to get him on his own.

He wasn't interested in the least, so the come-ons would go nowhere.

Not only was he only interested in one woman — and right now she was otherwise occupied and he'd hardly had time to talk to her — but he had pressing matters on his mind.

Matters relating to the footprint in Jess's garden border. That and his suspicions about the flying brick meets window scenario. It made him mad that someone would stoop so low. Someone who he suspected was more irked at him than Jess but was prepared to play the 'drama' card rather than be a man and come right out with it.

Ben Logan had made no mystery of the fact he didn't like Gabe but taking revenge and damaging property wasn't a gentlemanly way to solve a grievance of any kind. Not that he had proof. Yet.

But he had suspicions.

And the print was being followed up by the police now. He hoped it would prove his hunches correct.

Gabe peered into the darkening pub garden looking for a giveaway glimpse of Jess but she was nowhere to be seen.

The tables on the garden's deck were deserted and the local pub regulars had fled tonight to escape the busy party booking.

'Jess?' Gabe called into the darkness as a lone owl hooted back as his only reply.

He'd seen her after she'd been out here talking with Dr Logan. She'd come back into the party briefly and presented Ruth with some comedy gifts and then disappeared again.

He wished she'd take it easier.

Maybe she'd gone home? Back to

soap-making or whatever she did in her office late at night, the angle-poise lamp low, her head bowed, silhouetted in the lit window. Yes, he'd watched. Whenever he'd got the chance.

She was like a guilty pleasure that slowly warmed, mellowed and brought you back for a bigger indulgence. He liked the buzz she gave. Her smiles, her come-backs. He craved her company and she was getting too addictive for comfort.

Gabe buttoned his denim jacket unacustomed to Scotland's chill night air. He walked around the side of the inn and saw the waterfront shimmer through dancing trees at dusk.

Invergarry was stunning, the sun now setting on the loch like a mystical orb on a midnight velvet cushion. The urge to paint made his fingers itch. He saw the last golden rays of sunset glimmer and silhouette Jess Gilmour perfectly, down by the loch.

Gabe smiled. He hardly knew her, but already, he did at heart.

She made his insides warm and heat simultaneously.

She made him have faith in the world around them and he didn't know why.

Gabe started towards her. Not knowing yet what he'd say when he got there. Just knowing he had to go.

★   ★   ★

'Jess. It's Gabe.'

His voice was quiet and smooth. But when she turned and saw how good he looked in the dappled fading light it unnerved her completely and she was unable to reply.

She'd hoped to evade everyone; start afresh tomorrow.

Her mind was too full right now for anything but isolation. Ben Logan wanted to be her partner in Rowan Croft Holidays. She still couldn't take it in; hadn't seen it coming at all.

It freaked her out and unnerved her, probably a throwback from having a controlling husband once before. Could she really let a man into her affairs? Would she regret reneging independence that was so ingrained?

Having a solution to her cash flow problems pop up right in front of her was good — but it was also confusing. As unexpected as it was surreal. This could alter everything but could also help her enormously.

Would she be mad to pass it up? When she knew Ben already and it would cut out a long, arduous slog to find the right match for an investor.

So much for well laid plans.

Gabe watched her levelly.

'You're quiet. Sorry — am I disturbing you?'

She rubbed her arms to ward off the goosebumps. 'I'm just taking some time out to think.'

Gabe had come down here to find her when all she'd sought to do was creep away from the cacophony of the party to mull it all and give it time to settle. In truth, her mind was sprinting spirals wondering if she'd be mad to accept Ben's offer.

Or mad to turn it down.

She needed investment. She needed wriggle room in her schedule and on her bank ledgers. Ben was offering that on a plate. Offering what she needed. So why was she so confused?

He'd mentioned an investment sum that had surprised and impressed her. Dr Logan was clearly serious about investing his savings in a business venture and he had impressive capital to prove it.

Accepting what he'd offered would be an answer. A solution. And an immediate fix all rolled into one.

So what was keeping her from saying a speedy yes?

What had made her tell him she'd like some time to consider his proposal?

'You OK?' Gabe asked again. 'You're not, are you?'

Jess's heart drummed fast at the catch in Gabe's voice. She gulped before she answered him. 'I'm fine. Thanks for helping tonight. Sorry you must've felt like a lamb to the slaughter in that room of pawing women.'

'They're harmless.'

'You think?'

He grinned at her ruefully. 'Some more harmless than others. I think I have fingerprints on me from some of them.'

'Actually they're all asking me if you have a website. I think some of them thought I'd hired you as a stunt cowboy barman. They'll all be going to the library and hiring out *Gone With The Wind*.'

Gabe laughed. 'I'm no Rhett Butler. They're trying out the bronco machine now and it ain't pretty but Ruth's had a great night and you did her proud.'

His green eyes pierced hers. That killer dimple kicked in and she almost groaned. 'Didn't fancy bronco yourself?'

'I'm not that into parties,' Jess admitted. 'I do have good news for you, though. I had to visit Rhona, she's the

Chairman of the Art Club locally. Very highly regarded and she has a discerning eye. She loved your sketchbook — asked if you'd take a commission? Or even better, she'd be interested in having a few paintings for her forthcoming show.'

'You're not serious,' Gabe answered shortly. 'I can't believe you showed those foolish doodles to anyone.'

'Rhona thinks they have merit. And I think you're being overly modest. She'll probably seek you out soon. She seemed very keen.'

Gabe simply shrugged his shoulders. 'I could've gone to art school once. Turned down the opportunity. I always wanted to learn more — some said I had some talent. No use crying over might have beens, though. Anyway — why are you skulkin' here all on your lonesome?'

'Actually I've had a few surprises to think over tonight. It's left me a bit bewildered.'

'You don't have to tell me anything

you don't want to,' said Gabe matter-of-factly, but Jess simply shrugged.

'It's OK. Nothing confidential that can't be aired. The investor meeting today was a wash-out. Not the kind I'd want to pursue. But I've had surprise interest from another party — let's just say somebody local known to us both has offered me a lot of money to become a partner in the holiday lets side of my business. It's all been very unexpected — sudden — so I needed time to just sit and think.'

Gabe watched her carefully.

He looked like he was considering his words at length. He didn't say a word. Which surprised her so she probed him.

'Go on. Say something.'

'Let me guess . . . the man with the stethoscope and the stifling tendency to stalk your engagement diary?'

'You really don't like him, Gabe, do you?' she observed.

'From what I've seen so far he's done nothing to recommend himself. This just underlines my concern.'

'Don't Gabe. It's business — not personal. Ben's not such a bad guy. He just sometimes doesn't present himself in the best light.' Jess watched the last rays of sun dance off the lapping water. It smelled of juicy foliage and shingle and woodland. If only her fired senses would sharpen her decision-making process.

Gabe shook his head. 'Not showing himself in a good light — and that's such a great personality trait in a business partner.'

Jess felt irritation slice inside her at Gabe's instant negativity. 'I don't tend to judge people in as black and white a light as you. You make snap decisions on people's characters in Texas?'

'All I'm saying is take your time.' She saw his jaw flex in the falling light. She also saw him kick his boot in the shingly sand. She'd noticed before he did that when he was spoiling to say something controversial or make his point known.

'Of course you realise it's a cover. It's a fresh offensive to get your attention. A behind the back stab at me. Bottom line is Ben Logan has the hots for you and he's decided he's going to win at all costs.'

'That's ridiculous!' Jess refuted.

Gabe challenged. 'Is it? Can you be so very sure?'

'Anyway, this is not about you!' Jess added, feeling annoyance rile her.

OK, she had reservations herself but that didn't give Gabe Garrett the right to steam in with his prejudices and assumptions and knock down the only walls of opportunity with foundations worthy of consideration. She so badly needed some leeway and some business support — accepting this offer would be a gift from the Gods.

But Gabe rattling on the chains of her uncertainty only managed to make her angry.

'You two are worse than fighting grizzly bears. It's ridiculous. You both need to grow up!'

'I'd rather deal with a grizzly than Dr Logan. At least they can have a charming side. Personally I'd have gone for the rattlesnake comparison. That man is not to be trusted.'

'And you know this how?' Jess shoved her hands across her chest in defensive retaliation.

'Look. If it makes you say no to that man — I'd like to offer to match his investment myself.'

'Now you're being crazy. You're from Texas. What do you want shares in a tiny Scottish business for?'

'To make sure you don't make a bad relationship mistake, Jessica. That's what.'

She was shocked at his offer.

And his statement.

Of course she wasn't for a minute going to believe he actually meant it.

She moved further away from Gabe and shoved her hand through her hair as she struggled with the night's events. She didn't want to smell his scent. Didn't want to feel his mockery of her.

Didn't want to feel any more of a business failure than she already did.

'You're right. Let's not talk about this. It's my business so I should keep it to myself,' she concluded.

'You think he'd be an asset to you?' Gabe asked.

'He's respected locally, yes. He's a doctor with a thriving practice for goodness sake.'

'Respected. With his bedside manner?'

Jess shook her head and groaned. 'I don't even know why I'm discussing this with you when you've so clearly made your mind up.'

'You think he can bring value and merit — support you to achieve your aims?'

Jess shivered in the loch side breeze.

'I haven't really thought it through. But he's talking impressive figures. He's looking to invest and he figures the holiday let business would be like investing in property and an already established local set-up. The ideal way for him to dip his toe in the waters as an entrepreneur. He wants a fifty fifty share in the properties themselves.'

'I don't like the sound of it. What if you fall out down the line and he decides to sell the property from under your business? It's your business, Jess. Your grandmother's inheritance. Don't lose sight of that. I meant what I said. I'll match his bid.'

'My business needs money but there's no way I'm causing a bidding war between the two of you. The reserves are draining and the demands sky high. Having someone help shoulder some of my commitments would make a big difference.'

Gabe's mouth was a thin drawn line. 'So you think he's the perfect prescription for business health? An antidote to the recession? All I'd say is watch your step, and your back. I think his money comes with a price tag — he's using it to get closer to the real prize. He wants you and he might just be angling to get some prime local property at your expense at the same time.'

'That's ridiculous.'

'Is it?'

'Definitely.'

'I envy your faith in him,' Gabe said darkly and he turned away from her showing his disappointment. 'Then go ahead. Pursue it. But don't say I didn't warn you when it all comes crashing down around you and you wind up selling out to him — in the business sense and the personal one. I predict he's moving in — circling. Rattlesnake Logan needs careful watching.'

With that Gabe nodded and walked away without looking back.

* * *

When Jess got back to her cottage Gabe's was all in darkness.

She didn't know whether to feel glad he wasn't awake or annoyed that he could sleep so easy after their fight.

Had it been a fight?

Was he doing her a favour — stating all the secret misgivings she had lurking at the back of her brain about Ben Logan — or was he over-stepping every possible mark?

She already knew she probably wouldn't pursue Ben's offer. What experience did he have? What could he offer? And how could he really expect her to become a joint owner in the cottage her grandmother had been born in? No. She didn't like the fit of his proposals.

Nor did she like tying herself to a man who never seemed to get the message they'd never be an item.

Gabe was right.

So why did knocking on his door now and admitting it feel like a no-go? Why did it hurt inside that they'd quarrelled?

All Gabe Garrett had ever really done was look out for her . . . cared . . . made sure she thought through the consequences of her actions.

He may not have a right to judge or make his views known, but his heart was in the right place.

As she unlocked her cottage she glanced at Gabe's dark bedroom window.

She'd talk to him tomorrow.

And maybe — in a roundabout way — tell him she'd heard his views and listened. Even if saying sorry in so many words wasn't the plan.

9

'Hi there, great to see you. But . . . um . . . what are you doing here?' Ruth looked up from forking hay in her stables block the next day.

Jess was biting her lip and hoping for a mood-vent. She had woes on her mind that needed airing and what was a best friend for if not a mechanism for such therapy?

'I'm pretending to be at a meeting.'

'I hate to break this to you Jess but Pure Pleasures is your business. You can't pretend when you're the boss. It doesn't work out quite the same. Just leads to annoyed customers waiting outside.'

'Sheila's covering again. I need think time. A lot has been happening and it's left me in a bit of a whirl.'

'Good night last night?' Ruth grinned.

'Actually — it didn't go as well as I

might have hoped,' Jess replied. 'Though you had a good time, didn't you? That's all that matters really.'

'Immensely. Especially the entertainment — I broke a heel I danced so much. So what happened to you? I don't remember seeing you leave. Or seeing you master the bronco.'

Ruth was mucking out stables. Proof that as a stable owner you got on and did what needed to be done, even if she was going to be a bride in a matter of a few days.

'So what happened?' Ruth asked.

'Gabe and I had a big fight,' Jess answered.

'For a moment there I thought you were going to say you kissed!' Ruth winked and faked a nudging gesture.

Jess bit her lip and then slumped down on a pile of feed bags in the corner then drew both hands over her face. The horse in the next box looked up at her with wary eyes.

'Spill,' Ruth said softly. 'Can't be that bad? Let me guess. You like each other really but you're both trying to hide it so arguing became the next available outlet?'

Jess put her chin on her knees and slowly explained about Ben's offer and Gabe's outrage and disappointment; his grim predictions and his stormy walk off.

'Is that it?' Ruth stood frowning. 'You just need to kiss and make up.'

Jess stared hard at her friend. 'He's mad at me!'

'And you're hiding from him. You're both acting like kids and you need to sit down and talk like adults instead. He likes you. And you like him, whether you're admitting it to yourself or not.'

See, that was the thing about Ruth. There was no messing with her. She was the best friend who went straight for the jugular and the bottom line.

'He's a guest. He's from Texas and I never do flings,' Jess said softly as if that explained everything.

'And Josh was from Texas. And I didn't do flings either. Sometimes a girl makes exceptions. Good ones.'

Jess screwed up her nose. 'But he's going to be related to you and I can barely think straight when he's around. If I see him again I'll only end up in a heap of mush. Everything he says to me sends me in circles and I can barely stand to be in the same room as him when we're alone because he makes me feel so special . . . vulnerable . . . confused. Oh heck, Ruth. I've never been like this before.'

'You do have it bad, sweetie,' Ruth said and reached out to brush her friend's hand.

'So I'm using good sense and putting distance between us. That way we'll both survive the wedding. We just need to be sensible and remember nothing can happen.'

'No — that's not it at all. Don't blame my wedding. It's the two of you at close quarters and renegade hormones that are to blame. Isn't it about time you went and found a life? Grabbed some romance?'

Jess gaped at Ruth in a goldfish impression.

'You're supposed to tell me I'm being wise and prudent.'

'Do you want to live like a nun forever, Jess Gilmour?' Ruth said raising her eyes to her friend. 'You're running scared but that's hardly surprising given your past with Dan. Have you even seen Gabe today to break the ice? Do you realise the way he watches you? Just talk things through and take it from there.'

'I can't. I have a meeting in Drumaber later.'

Ruth shrugged and shook her head.

'He's talked about you incessantly since he got here. Josh and I noticed. I think attraction's been bleeping in both your ears for the past week. And that's normal, you're both grown ups and it's even more OK to admit it. In fact it's nice. I'd love to be related to you. Now that he's mellowed, I figure he's a very sexy proposition. You'd be crazy to walk away, Jess.'

'Argh.' Jess suddenly jumped from her seat. Inner frustration was ramping up inside her. It wasn't like her to feel this powerless and it wasn't OK to do this for the pure entertainment of others.

'I'm not starting an affair. And by the way, this is strictly private so no telling anyone. Period.'

'Too late, sweetie. Most of Invergarry have already noticed. I'd say there's been smoke signals for days. Primarily because a few females took a liking to muscle-bound Gabe, your manual slave. They assumed you were an item. So we're all hoping for a finale. What are you going to do about the row?'

Ruth shoved her pitch fork in the wheelbarrow.

'Avoiding further engagement.'

Ruth approached her and held her gaze steady. 'You can't avoid men forever. Is this about the wedding? Is it hard for you, bringing back memories of Dan? Because if that's what's really at the root here, you just have to say.'

It wasn't Dan. Not in a million eons. She'd firmly bolted that trapdoor shut. Her marriage was a dim memory and she was glad to have it behind her. But it did flag up a need for supreme caution.

When she'd first met Dan it had been a whirlwind romance with no thought of good sense. A crazy, high-speed flirtation and a quick engagement for them both. Life had taught her that a calm head served well.

Jess shook her head vehemently. 'My marriage isn't remotely comparable to you and Josh and I'm over the moon that you're getting married. This is about me. Keeping things sensible with Josh's brother.'

Ruth moved closer and Jess rose to hug her friend. 'Sure?'

'Positive.'

It was only then that Jess realised she'd been hugging a woman who'd been mucking out stables. She stepped back and brushed herself down.

'You're my best friend so of course I

back you. I still think you need to talk and admit how you both feel, though.'

Jess let out a deep internal sigh. 'Maybe. If only I knew the answer to that.'

Ruth added, 'No frostiness on my big day.'

Jess saluted her friend.

She knew Ruth was right; she'd have to face him sometime. At least she had an escape route for now and tonight she'd come back with a clear plan and a clearer head — if not a clear conscience.

Now wasn't the time to admit to Ruth that she still had over a hundred hand-made baby wild heather soap wedding favours to make — intricate, time consuming work that needed to be complete so that they could be dropped off next day at the hotel for the imminent wedding.

Jess kept that to herself.

It was one thing falling out with Gabe but she didn't want to cause upset to the bride, too!

Gabe arrived last — his brother and Nancy were already in the private room at The Crofter's. He'd reserved it for their meeting claiming it was a pre-wedding family gathering. Nobody need know anything about why they'd really arranged such a hasty, emergency family group.

He had thought things through long and hard.

He had it all planned out in his mind and now he just needed consensus.

'I want to invest in Pure Pleasures,' said Gabe frankly, his lashes skimming his cheeks as he checked the notepad before him. He had bags under his eyes from the sleepless night. He'd felt like the world was on his shoulders since last night's walk off. He wished he could rewind and put things right.

Gabe pushed forward a single sheet of A4 paper with some handwritten basic noted details scrawled over it.

Josh's sharp green eyes met his immediately.

'Wow. Does Jess know about Gold-Well Inc — is that what this is about? Did you admit the truth? Ruth has never imparted any real facts about the Garrett legacy to Jess. We always have stuck to the rule; no divulging outside of the family.'

'Of course she doesn't know about the company. Or the oil field. Or that we secretly own one of the richest bits of Texas in the state,' said Gabe getting testy. 'She thinks I'm a ranch guy with a chip on my shoulder.'

'You were when you got here,' Nancy added dryly. Gabe ignored her on purpose.

'Look, can we quit the cabaret? She thinks I paint fences and ride horses all day.'

'You do,' said Josh. 'Badly.'

Gabe narrowed his eyes. 'And I also back college funds. And arrange bursaries. And support care homes. And hospices. And fund school programmes.

You know the list — why are we doing this exactly?'

'Just to annoy you,' Nancy quipped. 'I love it when you're all worked up like this.'

'Thank you little sister.' Gabe sighed heavily. 'Jess Gilmour has no idea about our wealth and our interests in Dallas. I wouldn't do anything without asking consent — I'm proposing we make an anonymous venture capitalist offer as sleeping partners. Jess needs investment and backing and she needs it fast. She's been let down and she's currently seeking a backer. She's had an offer from someone I deem unsuitable — I'm trying to make sure she has the best offer possible. I figure this is a good investment opportunity.'

Nancy was smiling from ear to ear.

'And what's so funny?' Gabe barked.

Nancy started to laugh again. Gabe wasn't feeling good. He'd spent a lousy night tossing and turning in bed. A night cursing himself for his argument with Jess and working out how he'd put it right. In the end he hadn't been able to because Jess had been absent from the store on a work errand all day.

It had all curdled inside him uncomfortably.

And somewhere around 2 a.m. he'd realised there was only one solution — offer Jess the money she needed. Make it anonymous and generous and give her the support she so genuinely deserved for her prized business to flourish. And do it fast.

Out manoeuvre the rattlesnake.

Take that, Dr Stethoscope! The best man just won!

'Agreed?' Gabe checked. 'I can have the arrangements worked out, documents drawn up and a firm offer made — anonymously of course, via Jess's accountant with an assurance of confidentiality and anonymity — in the minimum of time.'

'Of course we're agreed,' said Josh. 'I can't believe you took me out of morning surgery for this. I have a queue of people waiting to have their pets inspected and treated. You could've done this easily without having this crazy secret meeting with coded messages summoning us here.'

Nancy was still smiling. Even her shoulders were moving as she stifled the giggles.

Suddenly Gabe was feeling really annoyed and irritated.

'What's with the grinning, sister?'

'You. You've got it bad. Worse than I ever suspected.'

Gabe began to slightly raise his voice. He wasn't usually the shouty type but weariness and anxiety were fuelling this new alter ego. 'Don't be crazy. It's business. It's called supporting a friend in need. Jess and Ruth are like family now.'

'What a turnaround from the man who didn't want to come to Scotland!' Nancy's eyes sparkled as she teased and accused her older brother.

'All I want is a yes vote. Do I have it from you both, or do I have to lasso you and tie you to the chair?'

'You have my yes,' said Nancy rising from her seat. 'Jess gets my vote. And you, my dear brother, most definitely have it bad. You're in love with her — and you don't even realise it!'

10

Jess stood up and stretched her aching back. She'd only done ten favours and already her fingers were starting to get sore. She'd have a long, long night ahead.

She normally loved the tiny, delicate place favours for every wedding guest. It felt like having the privileged task of producing a very personal memento to a most special day.

If only she'd slept better.

And not worried all day.

If only she'd ironed out her problems with Gabe Garrett sooner instead of ducking responsibilities and playing hide and seek from her conscience.

Jess looked at the large baskets of wares that still needed to be made into finished favours. So tiny, so time-consuming. She should enjoy this — they were for her very best friend in the world. Beautiful ornate miniature Celtic scroll soaps and tiny magic potion sized bottles of Eternal Love body lotion. Each hand packed into tiny parchment boxes filled with dried rosebuds and tied with a silk tartan ribbon and a dried sea lavender posy.

Tonight she just wasn't in the mood.

Her phone buzzed in her pocket and she felt grateful to have something else to think about. She scanned its screen.

Hi. Can I come in please if I say I'm very sorry and promise not to do it again? read the text on her phone.

The sender was Gabriel Garrett.

The urge to smile bubbled inside her as she re-read the words.

Come in. With your white flag and olive branch at the ready, she typed in reply.

A couple of moments after the text was sent the door opened slowly. He came in clutching an enormous bunch of exquisite bespoke flowers in his arms, his characteristic smile replaced by a sombre expression.

Behind the flowers there was a bottle of champagne too.

'Gabe! I'm the one who should be apologising.'

'Let's not do this. Just take the olive branches and put them in some water. Actually — stay there. You look busy. I already know where your vases and buckets are, remember?'

He walked through the shop to go to her workshop.

At least he smiled when he presented her with the flowers, she thought, watching him return.

'Can we be friends again?' he asked softly.

'Who says we weren't?'

'Me. I stuck my big cowboy boots into your business.'

'And I turned into The Independent Iron Lady. Sorry, Gabe.'

'Mutual truce?' he ventured.

She nodded her agreement. 'Thanks for the bubbly. And the flowers — they're amazing!'

They were. The bouquet must've cost

a fortune. It was an armful of exquisite, arty, tropical blooms; they were gorgeous.

'You were right,' she said softly lowering her nose to enjoy the scents of the flowers in her arms, hand-tied and encased in tissue and wrappings. 'Ben isn't the right match for my business.'

'That's not for me to comment on.'

'But he isn't. So you were right. I just sometimes don't like the truth being said out loud. I like to think I come up with all the answers myself.'

Gabe Garrett stood before her and put down his vases of water. Then he smiled and she realised that she'd missed that smile. Worried about never seeing it again. Hated that they'd got so over-heated and annoyed over somebody who didn't deserve the accolade.

'On that you're not alone. So . . . what do you want me to do to make it up to you?' Gabe asked. 'Wear a hair shirt? Mop the floor; sleep on a bed of nails? Name your desire?'

'Actually,' said Jess having a brain-wave which would not only help her out but allow her to spend some time with Gabe rebuilding their relationship.

'Don't suppose you fancy helping me make wedding favours . . . they're honestly not as tricky as they look.'

Gabe looked around him then unbuttoned his shirt sleeves and rolled them up to reveal a very fine set of tanned, muscular forearms. 'Won't promise I'll be good at it, but I'll give it my best shot if it means I can stay here and distract you for the rest of the evening!'

★   ★   ★

Gabe Garrett surprised himself.

He not only managed to make a mean wedding favour — pretty too as well as accurate and fast — but he also managed to keep his secret to himself.

He itched to tell her his good news; that she was about to get the business solution she so badly needed and deserved. GoldWell Drillers Inc would be supporting her business and giving it the wings to fly, no strings attached.

But Gabe couldn't tell her that. He needed to keep his cover safe. He didn't tell people about his money — not since Marie had shot his faith in human nature to hell because of it. When he'd been a farm boy rancher he hadn't been enough for her. Then when he'd inherited oil wells and billions of dollars overnight she'd suddenly revised her view. It was enough to leave her man and arrive back at Broken Bridle on his doorstep with her one-year-old daughter and a long story about him being the only one for her.

It had firmed Gabe Garrett's resolve to keep his circumstances to himself. He'd never date or encourage a gold-digger. Nor would he assume people have decent underlying motives; even those he trusted.

'I need to tell you about something that happened today,' said Jess. 'You brought me flowers. I have something of a surprise for you myself.'

Gabe looked up from the row of tiny boxes they'd now completed, flexing his stiff fingers.

'I went to a gallery today — in Drumaber. It's a lovely town; really touristy with a gallery and art shop of some renown. Anyway — they want to stock your paintings. They bought all the art from your sketchbook. They asked if you'd supply more but I told them you were a guest of mine who's passing through.'

The light in his heart — the one Jess had just kindled and blown on and made burn bright and warm and rejuvenating — began to shutter and fade with the words 'passing through'.

That was how she saw him. A temporary aberration.

A cowboy she'd once met. One who painted and argued and helped her with manual tasks and then went back to the life of his own making.

Gabe watched her. Eyes aglow. Keenness all over her expression because she was so pleased for him.

'Thank you, Jess.'

'You see. You are good. The gallery says so, and the Chair of the Art Club, and they all know their stuff. I knew it wasn't just me making more out of it than you'd let me. You've talent, Gabe Garrett. You need to recognise that and do something with it.'

He wanted to kiss her.

He watched her lips, itching to make good his inner desires.

He saw her bubble with enthusiasm and honesty. If he could bottle Jess Gilmour's energy and take home her rare spark, he would. And he'd never let her go.

'I'm not properly trained.'

'Then you should pursue it.'

'How — I have a lot of commitments back home.'

'You told me to re-prioritise. Why can't you do the same?'

Because I'm scared of failing again. Like I did with Marie.

I'm scared of trusting a woman

224

who'll let me down.

Because I'm a man with more money than I could ever spend in a lifetime. But I can't buy love.

How on earth could he go to art school with a bunch of young adolescent students . . . those days had passed him by.

Or had they?

'I guess I'll have to think about that,' said Gabe. 'You've given me lots to think about, Jess. So very much.'

And that's when the cowboy code went to Timbuktu.

Gabe threw the rulebook and good sense to the four winds and went with his gut instinct.

He reached his hand out and drew Jess to him with just the gentlest touch of his palm and a flick of his finger. In moments his mouth was next to hers, she was in his arms, and he was kissing her like cowboys in songs in movies ought to.

Gabe Garrett had finally followed his inner instinct to take his woman in his arms and show her how much she meant, and it felt so right.

★ ★ ★

It wasn't a dream. She was willingly in the arms of Gabe Garrett and it had just somehow happened.

His passionate kiss was too good to be imaginary, taking her breath away with its power and intensity. She felt his strong but gentle hands in her hair; his thumb stroking the nape of her neck. She was quivering in places that hadn't stirred in a very long time.

'Gabe.'

'Shhh. You'll break the spell,' he murmured.

Gabe's sexy green eyes bored into hers. He had the sweetest smile. 'Sorry. Guess I lied. I am more interested in distracting you than finishing the job in hand.'

'And you told me you always uphold the cowboy code. What about work ethic and attention to detail.'

'Didn't anybody ever tell you a cowboy always gives the prettiest girl in the room priority attention?'

Jess smiled. 'You really kissed me, Gabe Garrett,' she whispered. 'Oh my.'

'I've wanted to for so long,' he whispered, unwilling to relinquish his hold on her.

'And I have a confession to make. I came here tonight because I wanted to spend time with you.' He shrugged broad shoulders. 'I'm only interested in one woman. She has a great head for business. She makes great soap. And she's caught my attention since the day I came here.'

'But Texas is a long way from my world,' Jess said softly, not wanting to break the easy intimacy between them, but knowing someone had to add a dose of reality to their conversation. 'We shouldn't have kissed. It could get messy.' She let go of him.

'Who cares when it feels this good?' he said, stepping towards her again. 'You can't be rational all your life.'

'Sometimes we can't afford not to be rational and practical.'

'Trust the guy who got things all wrong when our mother died, and got annoyed with his brother for leaving the ranch — I know irrational when I see it,' Gabe said.

'I'm sorry about your mother,' Jess said softly. Then she asked. 'Did she suffer long?'

'She spent time in a hospice and died after a long battle with dementia.' Gabe's tone grew soft. 'Josh found it hard and I think that made him hate Texas. He watched all the changes in Mom and home wasn't the same.'

'I'm sorry for your loss, Gabe. Josh doesn't hate Texas. Don't keep thinking that way.'

'He loves Scotland more.' Gabe shrugged and Jess didn't comment. 'Can't compete when there's a woman as beautiful as Ruth who's stolen his heart,' Gabe added.

'You're way too hard on yourself,' she said softly. 'It's not about you. It's about them being head over heels in love with each other. Nobody can compete with that.'

Jess realised Gabe Garrett had weathered storms. He wasn't a bad man. He was weathering another one and managing to make it through the chaos. Maybe what he'd suffered already was one of the reasons behind his difficulties with the wedding?

'Jess Gilmour, I've never felt like this. You make me feel like my skin's on inside out — I can't think straight for wanting to be with you.'

Jess stared. Blinking at what he'd just said.

'I want to get closer but I'm scared I'll scare you off. And I'm terrified that if I don't do something I'll regret it.'

'But I have baggage, and mine makes me reluctant to voyage near relationship territory again,' Jess confided so softly it was a whisper. She shivered just saying the words out loud. Her past still had the power to make her cold and summon the dark clouds over her day.

'Honey, we all have pasts. I had a woman in my life once; it all went wrong and it wasn't an experience I want to repeat. I don't have a great pedigree but it doesn't make me afraid to try again. Not when I feel like this.'

Gabe put up a hand to cup her chin and make her look at him. He stared at her with dark, sparkling eyes.

'You attract me so hard it has me scrabbling for sanity. You say things that make straight sense and when you smile at me my insides hurt with wanting to kiss you. But I won't push you, I can see you're still hurting from your own loss.'

Pain flashed across Jess's face.

'My husband didn't deserve the mourning. Turns out Dan had a girlfriend in Spain. The business trips weren't restaurant related. He had a pretty active sex life and he'd set her up in a tapas bar. He had more ambition than I'd realised and it involved another woman. And all the while I stayed home and balanced his books . . .'

How did you begin to explain that your husband had a mistress who only emerged via credit card transactions and an extra mortgage she'd never known about? If he hadn't died, she may never have known. How long would he have continued leading a double life?

Gabe stared hard at her but only emitted a sorry sigh.

'It's what makes me work so hard. To prove I can do better. The man I trusted wasn't worth it so the biggest fool was me. I was hoping to avoid you because I don't have space in my head to let you in, Gabe. I can't trust any man again. Not Dan. Not Ben. Not even you.'

The stream of past hurts was suddenly in full flow. Big mistake. She inwardly cursed the small glass of champagne she'd had earlier while they'd sat and chatted.

'He didn't deserve you. Jess, it doesn't have to be this way.' Gabe stared at her earnestly. 'So you don't like me?' Gabe baited.

'I didn't say that.'

'You hate Stetsons. You can't stand horses. And you'd never be seen on a ranch or watching a western movie in your life?'

She fixed him with a chastening stare.

'This is just an out of character mistake for you,' he prompted. 'No chemistry at play at all?'

Jess shook her head. What could she say — admitting that there was seismic chemistry between them would only fuel his pursuit. Sadly — as much as she liked Gabe and craved his attention — pursuit was not a realistic objective.

'It was a kiss and we're consenting adults, Miss Jessica. I don't see what's so wrong with that.'

What kind of havoc was he unleashing here?

Jess's cell phone buzzed in her pocket and she scrambled to put it the right way round. She saw it read Ruth's number and rather than put herself in the dilemma of having to talk to her best friend and pretend to be normal, she switched it off completely.

She stared at the phone rather than looking at Gabe but he side-stepped her tactic by placing a long finger under her chin and raising it to make her watch him.

Oh, how she wished she was braver, wished he wasn't just a passing stranger. She couldn't just follow passion's lead. She'd already fallen hook, line and sinker for him but couldn't admit that to anyone; not even herself.

★   ★   ★

It was almost as if the kiss had been a dream after all because nothing more was ever said or done about it.

Suddenly wedding preparations were stepped up and put on fast forward.

Surely that was the reason why she and Gabe were busy, distracted, hardly sharing two words together? They weren't just awkward, regretful and unsure of how to handle things, were they?

Surely they were just caught up in wedding fever — it wasn't the kiss that had made him bolt?

Jess bit the very edge of her lip as she sat in her accountant's office, then stopped herself — a bridesmaid with ragged bitten lips would not be a very nice addition to the wedding photographs.

She had so much to do. She'd promised to help Ruth with a million and one tasks and she still had the businesses to run. And now Archie Haverstock had called her in saying it was vital he see her. When he'd told her the news she'd almost felt faint.

'An anonymous venture capitalist. Their credentials really are exceptional and the money can be wired as soon as you sign the documents. They're very keen and see great potential in your business. Their terms are fair. It's just what you dreamed of, Jess. This will enable you to take on staff. Open new stores. The sky's the limit, Jess. You can go ahead and make strategic developments to the core business.'

It was clear Archie was excited.

She was too. But she was also numb.

Not that it wasn't good news — it was great and she wanted to share it and sing it to the rafters. So what made her want to call Gabe first? And what made her regret that since the kiss they'd both backed off . . .

Gabe had become reticent. Distant and quiet.

She'd matched his moves. Even though it was for the best, it didn't make it easier to handle.

It was as if she'd woken up on Christmas morning and been given the world and everything in it, only to find out that she really didn't care for such lavishness and would prefer her old discarded toys instead.

Not that Gabe Garrett could ever be considered a discarded toy. He was everything she couldn't have — but everything she wanted.

The stern, boring business woman inside her, the widow who'd been bitten and burnt before, refused to let her even consider for a moment that wanting him might be an option.

No, Gabe was definitely off limits and he clearly felt that way about her too.

'So you're happy?' said Archie. 'Going to sign?'

'Yes, delighted,' said Jess picking up her pen. 'I'd be a fool to turn this down. It's everything I could ask for.'

If only I could have the Texan cowboy too, she thought.

★   ★   ★

With one day to go until the wedding, Jess was definitely avoiding him. In truth he'd been in turmoil himself.

He'd had business to deal with from Dallas. It had taken time, phone conferences and careful thought. He'd holed himself away in Rowan Croft to get things dealt with.

By the time he'd finished, when he'd seen Jess, things had definitely been stilted and awkward.

How many best men managed to alienate the maid of honour by the big day?

Gabe had tried to talk to her — post kiss. She'd been polite; made short replies to his small talk. He could tell he'd freaked her out and made her back into her emotional snail's shell.

Who could blame her?

And what bothered him most of all — she didn't even make a big deal of announcing her news. If she'd signed the contract for the investment, she'd chosen not to share it.

That hurt, like a rattlesnake strike from nowhere.

⋆   ⋆   ⋆

Josh was chatting to Ruth on his cell phone when Gabe got there. He hadn't asked to come over and had just turned

237

up uninvited. It was the night before the wedding after all; the eve of a very big day — he figured his brother might need a pep-talk and support.

The sound of their muted laughter and intimate tone caused something to curl in Gabe's stomach. For once he wished he had that too — someone who'd burn all the woes away with a fond kiss or a whispered endearment.

Gabe discreetly wandered around the garden at the back of Josh's croft-style cottage while they finished the call.

'Hi, brother,' Josh said flipping shut his phone. Josh motioned for him to sit down at the wooden bench set that sat on the cobblestone patio.

'You OK?' asked Gabe.

'Sure. Can't wait for tomorrow to come. It's you I'm worried about, though.'

'Me?'

'You may not realise this Gabriel, but it's just as well you've never played cards because your poker face would have you destitute. You're in a mess. I can read it and sense it. So why don't you start at the beginning and tell me what it's all about? Jess, isn't it?' Josh laid a hand on his arm.

'She isn't speaking to me. Well . . . that's not true. She's speakin'. Bein' civil . . . but it's faked. I can sense it. And it's eatin' me up inside.'

'Jess is a good woman,' Josh confirmed. 'She accepted the money. She did the right thing.'

'I thought she'd be celebrating. There's been nothin' said. I don't even know if she's taking up the deal yet.' Gabe looked nonplussed.

'She is,' Josh answered. 'She told Ruth she'd signed the papers.'

Gabe sighed hard and paced.

'Why won't she talk to me? For the first time since we got into GoldWells I'm tempted to come out and admit who I am and what I do. I've always kept it quiet.'

'You want to tell her?'

'I want her to be secure and get the chances she deserves. She's got what she needs now. I just wanted her to be happy,' Gabe said.

'I'm guessing you also got the kiss the whole village has been putting wagers on?' Josh said softly then turned his eyes on his pacing brother.

Gabe stared at him incredulous.

Then he realised; who was he trying to kid. He put his hand through his hair.

'Enough kisses to turn a guy's head, but she doesn't feel it like I do. Which brings me to something else. I was wrong; you and Ruth are meant to be — you've found the dream. You followed your heart and let your spirit guide your life choices.' Gabe shook his head and looked around. The mountains were visible from here because in Invergarry there was amazing mountain views almost everywhere you looked.

'You did it. I hated you and blamed you and figured you were the one walking out on responsibilities — I should've been staring hard at myself. I have all that money for any cash investment possible and I've never, ever worked out what big emotional investment is needed to set me free.' Gabe hung his head. 'I've been a fool. I'm sorry. I did you wrong and I apologise.'

Josh blew out a long breath.

'There's nothing to be sorry about. You're my brother — we're all human and we all make assumptions sometimes. And mistakes . . . '

'I saw you and Ruth on the boat and wondered — did you think I was jealous? Have you all been figuring Gabe's got sour grapes because Marie went away and he didn't go after her quick enough? He turned down the art school course but she went anyway. And then she came back pregnant — and figured I'd be a wealthy surrogate daddy for her baby so she came back to good old Gabe . . . but all she wanted was my money. So I walked; turned my back again. I don't hold a torch for Marie — we were over and I'm over her.'

'To be honest,' Josh admitted, 'I had

no idea why you were so mad at me being here. Other than leaving the ranch. I knew I'd upset you but I didn't know how to make it better.'

'Momma made it hard,' said Gabe. 'I took all the difficult decisions. Like getting her nursing care and then a hospice . . . all while you were busy making travel plans. And Momma hated the fact that Marie went and I let her go. The ranch fell to me. Momma's disappointment fell to me, too. God knows I'd never resent giving my time to Momma. I took responsibility for the ranch because that's what everyone expected. I turned Marie away when I realised she just wanted the best financial deal she could get. It was only the Garrett's big money windfall that brought her back. It's why I've stayed a rancher hermit. I vowed I'd never let the money change me; I'm still just Gabe from Broken Bridle Ranch.'

Josh moved closer to his brother and stretched an arm around his shoulder.

'I'm sorry you felt isolated and

dumped on, Gabe. And Marie wasn't the one for you.'

Gabe nodded sadly.

'Marie's old history.'

'Most of us figured Tall Trees Creek was what you wanted. You're the boy raised to run the ranch. What's brought all this on, brother?' Josh asked. 'All this blamin' yourself — because as far as I'm concerned I regret the feudin' and I just want you to be as happy as I am.'

'Jess,' said Gabe softly. 'She's made me see that ignoring things isn't the way. Duty isn't always well placed.'

Josh stared so hard at him, Gabe wondered if he'd spooked him out.

'Feel like I'm buttin' my head against a stone wall. She says she can't let a man into her life, just like I won't walk away from ranchin' . . . '

Gabe rose and paced the garden. 'Makes me see I've been ridiculous too,' he admitted. 'I need to face walkin' away from Broken Bridle for a life that I might like better.'

'You wanna leave? Try something

new?' Josh quizzed.

'Thinking so. I have a hankerin' to try.'

Was he crazy? Was Scotland putting mad notions in his addled, out-of-his-comfort-zone brain?

'You followed your heart. It worked,' Gabe said emphatically.

'And is Jess the one? Does Jess Gilmour mean everything?'

Gabe shrugged. 'All Jess wants is her business. I don't figure in her picture. Though I wish I did. God knows I want to. But no . . . I have to find my way. Now's the time.'

It had taken the loss of his mother and the emigration of his brother to prove to him that there was more to life than duty and loyal work-ethic.

'You think I'm failing Broken Bridle?' he asked Josh outright.

'Sounds to me like the only one you're failin' is yourself. Take a sabbatical, brother, do whatever it takes.'

And now Gabe felt like a subborn

idiot for taking so long to see it.

'You found happiness your way, maybe I can too. Though I've no idea what that is yet,' Gabe confided, feeling lighter already.

If only Jess Gilmour was coming back to Texas with him to help him find that direction he craved. But he guessed nobody could really have it all — even a secret billionaire.

11

Invergarry Castle was a lavish setting and the wedding promised to be as fairytale romantic as Scotland could get.

The arrival of the bride, ascending down the castle chapel's central aisle, caused a lump to wedge in Gabe's throat. His Mom would have been so proud of her middle child.

Outside, when Gabe and Josh had arrived, the saltire flag fluttered from the castle ramparts. The red carpet had been laid as a surprise too. There was a kilted piper playing by the entrance to the kirk.

All the trimmings, and all of the touches, had been laid on for a very special day.

Gabe stood shoulder to shoulder with his brother awaiting the bride. The harpist's lilting version of *Highland*

Cathedral was just the right touch.

Hearing it, it was hard to leash his barricades. Especially when Ruth clutched her father's frail arm and the beaming man smiled his proud joy. Josh stood beside him, not yet daring to look back for the arrival of the bride.

Gabe whispered, 'Josh Garrett. You're one lucky guy.'

Ruth looked magical in her off-white silk dress, understated yet beautiful for the restraint. Gabe vowed he would not have regrets or thoughts about Tall Trees Creek or the past today. This day was Ruth and Josh's day alone.

Then Gabe spotted her maid of honour. Jess Gilmour walked behind the bride in a vivid pink silk dress that told amazing secrets about that body he'd held in his arms, the one she kept so well under wraps.

He was gifted with a hesitant smile just before Ruth reached her fiancé and the ceremony began.

He could not find sufficient words to

say anything at all. Mostly because he itched to touch that sloping curve of Jess's alabaster neck. Her words were replaying in his mind — her sentiments about holding onto special memories.

He figured this one would replay and keep him smiling for a long time to come.

His brother had made himself a future.

★　★　★

Jess quashed the impact of Gabe's appearance yet again. She watched him go up for seconds from the buffet table during the reception banquet, schmoozing and impressing every female wedding guest as they all helped themselves to the delicious array of cold cuts and hot dishes.

And why wouldn't these women be impressed?

He was a cowboy. Exotic, unattainable, charm personified. Yet always slightly self contained and slightly quiet, brooding and aloof.

He was wearing his suited wedding finery and it made the tiny hairs on her arms stir just to watch how good he looked in it. In full wedding ensemble Gabe was spellbinding. Hard muscle encased to great effect; his white shirt and black tie gasp worthy. Strong legs worthy of a sportsman and broad shoulders that suggested he could ably compete in the local Highland games without breaking a sweat were the final touch of perfection.

Today he oozed relaxed confidence like she'd never seen in him before.

It made it all the harder. Since 'the kiss' they really hadn't talked. They'd evaded and avoided and it felt like she'd somehow lost a good friend through a very misjudged act.

It wasn't fair — to be that self assured and good looking and utterly unaware of it too, she cursed inwardly.

Jess wished he hadn't blown things apart and yet a serious part of her knew this was for the best. Her heart would be sorely affected if they'd yielded to a brief relationship only for Gabe to leave. At least this way it was only a mistaken kiss . . .

Jess tried to push away the sadness in her heart — sadness that Ruth's mother hadn't been here. She'd died two years before after a battle with Motor Neurone disease. Ruth's smiles were heartfelt; she didn't need maudlin thoughts to darken things with regrets, but Jess had no doubts her mother would be on her mind today.

Ruth and Josh so deserved this happy day; a deserving couple who'd weathered adversity and were following love's true course. Who'd found each other and travelled long miles for their happy ever after . . .

A soft voice broke into her thoughts. 'Mind if I join you?'

Before she could answer Gabe sat down next to her, his tie and collar sexily loosened, his formal jacket cast aside. They both watched silently as his sister-in-law and her new husband slowly mingled with the guests, hand in hand.

Gabe gently took her hand and looked deep into her eyes. 'We have to go join them soon when the dancing starts. You OK with that? Figure we can be civil for that long?'

Jess nodded, though it felt like a whole butterfly house of insects had taken flight inside her tummy at the mere suggestion of getting into a tight dance embrace to slow music with Gabe Garrett. Even on a dance floor in a crowded room full of onlookers he had that much potency.

'Gabe. I'm sorry about the other night.'

'No need to even mention it.' He shrugged.

She didn't know what else to say, so instead they sat in companionable silence.

After they'd watched the newlyweds dance, they were invited to join them. Gabe led her out to the dancefloor and the slow waltz passed as in a dream.

She enjoyed the feel of his arms around her; savoured those brief moments of promise because she knew it would be the last chance she would ever get.

'I'm sorry,' Gabe said softly next to her ear, taking Jess by surprise. 'If I upset you when I kissed you, I'm sorry. And if I got it wrong and overstepped in how I am with you, I'm sorry for that too. If I bossed you around . . . '

She silenced his words. 'Forgotten,' she answered and faked a smile. 'I'm sorry I'm sensible. It doesn't mean I don't have feelings for you, but it really would be unwise for us both. It's nice to know that we were both tempted but we both chose common sense.'

'I've watched you look amazing all day in that dress. Your sunny yellow one captured my attention. This one takes the cake and the sundae cherry too.' Gabe grinned. 'Ruth picked a worthy attendant. From where I'm watching you couldn't get better.'

Gabe looked at her with eyes that burned.

She did welcome his flattery. She did feel gorgeous but she still felt unequipped for him. He outstripped her capabilities in so many ways. Especially when he looked so good he caused her breathing to hitch in her chest.

Jess motioned to his suit. 'Your mother would have been very proud of you.'

Gabe's eyes creased at the corners even though his jaw tensed at the mention of his family.

'Josh would've made her proud. I'm the one who committed to the ranch because he owed it to his momma for prior disappointments.'

Jess looked at him quizzically. 'You're a good man, Gabe. I don't believe you ever disappointed her.'

'I did. I didn't marry a woman who wanted me. I let her walk away and my mother told me I'd done the wrong thing. Maybe I'm not so much the good reliable Gabe everyone thinks I am? Maybe going back home's gonna test everything too. It's time to make big life decisions.'

Gabe's dark eyes nailed hers, intense and probing. He shook his head but his eyes kept on hers.

'I think I have to sell Broken Bridle, Jess. For a while now I've wondered if working the ranch in Tall Trees Creek the rest of my life is really what I need and want. Coming here has shown me I need to move on.'

Jess stared right back at him. 'It's OK to change. Lots of people alter their life paths. It needn't be a bad thing.'

The couples finished their waltz and Ruth presented a wrapped parcel to Jess. And one for Gabe too. When Jess opened hers, her fingers shook still holding the ribbon — it was an exquisite bracelet from a bespoke Scottish silversmith. Gabe had been given a Celtic Scots drinking cup in solid silver. She much admired both thoughtful mementos.

Without further words, and with a

weighty lump in her throat, she hugged her friend tight. Then she returned with Gabe to the table. He stood up and cupped her elbow. 'Come with me? I want to speak to you. I have things I need to say and they're important.'

Jess spotted the sombre fire in his eyes.

She kept the bubbling excitement under control when she followed him but she had a feeling this was more about saying goodbye than saying he loved her. And somehow that bothered her much more than she'd ever expected.

Perhaps her feelings for Gabe were much deeper than she'd imagined?

★   ★   ★

Gabe led her by the hand to the castle library.

When he shut the door behind them he drew her into his strong, warm arms.

'I have to kiss you again. If I don't I know I'll regret it.'

Their lips met and she revelled in the exquisite sensation. Gabe Garrett wasn't just an experienced cowboy — he was a darn fine kisser too.

'Say if you don't want this?' he whispered.

'I want it.'

'I have no expectations of you. I can't offer you promises and my life is complicated right now . . . ' He hesitated, looking deep into her eyes. 'Do you want this as much as me or should I walk away? I've tried to back up and stay immune. It just hasn't worked.'

'Yes. I feel it too,' Jess confessed in a whisper.

His lips met hers again, intense and hungry, conveying feelings he couldn't put into words.

She wanted him more than breathing. More than anything. Every single cell of her body yearned for everything this man had to give. She couldn't even explain it. All she knew was that a raw chemical reaction

made up of hormones and phero-
mones and attraction dust made her
want Gabe Garrett, heart and soul.

A loud knock on the door inter-
rupted them.

Gabe groaned and Jess sighed.

'I'd better answer it. It could be
important,' she said, breaking free of
Gabe.

'More important than this? I seri-
ously doubt that.'

He relinquished his grip reluctantly
and Jess went to the door. A waiter
handed her a note.

The scribbled message was from
reception; it said there'd been an urgent
call for her from The Crofter's Flask
— which surprised her as all arrangements for today were in hand. Jess
merely sighed and put the note in her
satin purse.

'There's a call in reception. I have
to go and get that. But I'll come
back. Stay here — I promise I'll come
back. This conversation isn't over yet.'

'I'm waiting, honey. Count on it.'

A firm hand snagged Jess's wrist roughly and pulled her through a nearby door with a hard yank that made her gasp.

The grabbing hand wasn't gentle — it was rough and uncaring — making her stumble in her high heels and hit the wall with an indelicate thud.

Ben Logan was on the end of that grabbing arm. He looked displeased; menacing. Suddenly Jess knew her instincts about him had been completely right — he wasn't a man to be trusted or tolerated.

'Jessica. There you are. The things I've had to do to get you here,' he said. His tone was like a gaoler. Teasing, demonic.

'What are you doing here? Why aren't you back at the wedding dance?'

She'd seen Ben at the church and she knew he'd been invited, but she'd been keeping a low profile with him of late. She tried to shake his arm away. 'I have to go. I need to make a call.'

'No you don't. The note was phoney — had to get you here somehow.'

'It was you!' She'd sensed Ben wasn't pleased but she wouldn't be bullied just because he figured he held sway. She wouldn't be terrorised by him either.

'I needed to speak to you,' Ben said gruffly. 'An impossible quest thanks to an over-zealous best man who keeps monopolising your time. Who does he think he is anyway?'

Jess knew immediately Ben Logan had been drinking. A lot. He smelled of strong whisky and he was leering and swaying on the spot. His eyes looked rheumy. Distaste curdled inside her at being so close to him and the fact he still held her tight. She wanted to walk off, or alternatively to run, but still he twisted and held her wrist and showed no sign of letting go.

It wasn't a nice feeling being held like this and it didn't bode well. She suddenly wished Gabe was with her.

'Ben. I think maybe we should call

you a cab home?' She tried to sound encouraging when she felt far from it. 'Everybody likes a glass or two at a celebration but everybody has their limits . . . '

'I've reached my patience limit and given you more than enough time,' Ben snarled. 'I'm going nowhere without you. I've done so much to get your attention and what do I get for my trouble? Blanks.' He grimaced and yanked on her wrist again causing it to twist painfully.

She protested with a reactive yelp and her fight or flight fear reflexes kicked in inside her.

'Ben! You're hurting me.'

'I've been hurting plenty too, though you never notice — trying to make you listen and date me and instead you always wriggle free. It's about time you knew the full truth about that cowboy of yours. Mr Perfect — there are things you need to know about Gabriel Garrett. But foremost I'm annoyed with you for ignoring my business offer and turning your back on my plans. What was that about?'

'I've had other investments to consider. I've been busy — I do run a business, you know.'

'Don't flannel me, Jess. I know you've already signed an investment by an overseas backer for the soap shop. I know this because I know who made the offer. You're not quite as smart as you like to believe.'

Jess was not only confused but starting to feel creeped out at how much Ben Logan did know.

He was repeating confidential information; making assertions that were right. How could he know any of this? The only person who knew was her accountant — she hadn't even told the full details to Ruth.

And she really didn't like the snarly way Ben talked about Gabe. Right now she figured he not only had a drink problem, he clearly had a grudge that had gone way too far. If she could shake him off she'd alert reception and hopefully summon security to remove him. She didn't want Ben spoiling Ruth's most special day.

'Don't be ridiculous. You can't know anything about my private business affairs. This is just bluff and you know it. It also makes me realise I was right to turn you down.'

'But I do know it all. I know that you accepted a weighty investment from an anonymous backer. But unlike you, I know his real identity — or do you really know that it's Gabe Garrett and you're just playing along with it to nail yourself a billionaire husband! Is that why I'm not good enough — you're out for the biggest fish you can fry?'

'What are you talking about?' Jess scoffed. 'You're delusional as well as disturbing. Let go of my arm, Ben.'

He didn't. He just kept on the offensive and kept his grip ultra tight.

'Underneath all that Texan farm-boy rancher disguise — he's loaded. Billionaire big shot from Texas. He could buy a million businesses like yours and still not break a sweat. He's a billionaire — all the Garrett's are. They own an oil dynasty in Texas. He's your backer and you didn't even know. Does that make you clever — or foolish? I'm really not sure.'

'Get your hands off her and shut the hell up before my fist connects with your jaw, Dr Logan! You've said quite enough,' said a menacing, loud Texan drawl from behind them.

It was Gabe.

A Gabe Garrett who she really knew nothing about if Ben Logan was to be believed.

A Gabe who'd come into her life and befriended her, confided in her — yet never once told her the whole truth.

She watched Gabe staring at Ben like he was about to tear him limb from limb. Though confused, and totally out of her depth, the last thing Jess wanted was a fist fight as her most poignant memory from Josh and Ruth's Wedding Day.

'Stop this, both of you! There won't

be any fighting.'

'You're right, there won't,' Gabe said with menace. 'The police are coming to detain him for questioning for fraud. Not only is he the kind of man who'll happily damage property just to even a personal score — yes, it was him who broke the window — he's also guilty of phone hacking and trying to get credit card information via email hacking too. He's been tapping my private cell phone line for the last couple of weeks. I didn't realise doctors could be so devious.'

Jess stared at them both askance. This was escalating so fast she could barely keep up.

She turned to Gabe and confronted him. 'Is it true? Are you really my backer?'

'It's not that simple . . . '

'Tell me straight. Are you or are you not my anonymous business investor, Mr Garrett? Are you JR Ewing's apprentice like he said?'

Gabe watched her.

His green eyes glittered but they also ghosted away as he nodded and shrugged his assent.

'Nice of you to keep me in the dark.'

'I never lied.'

'You didn't tell me the truth either, Gabe! You did this to even the score with Ben. You're both as bad as each other — you just want to win at all costs!'

'It's not like that at all,' Gabe argued. 'Not in the least. This guy's a louse. Ben Logan only knows because he's tapped the phones of Ruth and Josh before. He suspected they were worth money when Ruth offered to fund a vital dialysis machine for a young boy at the local cottage hospital. Ruth bought it without quibble . . . and Ben's been trying to worm his way into a business partnership with Josh ever since. Josh has repeatedly turned him down. Lately he's just got more desperate now that his creditors are banging harder on his door. He's a man with big money issues.'

No sooner had Gabe finished his explanation than quick as a flash Ben lashed out at him and grabbed him by the shirt tie, yanking it so that Gabe fell forward and almost smashed into the panelled wall.

Seconds later Gabe had retaliated with a resounding punch to Ben's jaw that made him stumble and think again. He sat on the floor and nursed his bleeding lip and his jaw ache.

Gabe opened the door as two tall police officers strode forward and Gabe pointed his head towards Ben.

'I think this is the gentleman you've been looking for, officers,' he said.

*   *   *

Jess stepped back a pace as the police helped Ben to his feet. It felt like being in a very small space with rather a lot of people in it — and everything in Jess's mind was a blur. Confusion tinged with sadness.

Gabe hadn't told her the whole truth.

266

Yes, he'd bought a large stake in her business — but he'd done it the sneaky way. Was he out to defraud her too, lie and hurt her like her husband ultimately had?

Anger speared her and she had to rein in the instinct to lash out at him.

When she looked up, feeling dazed, Jess saw Nancy was beside her. She wore a shocked expression herself but said nothing. She clearly knew what had been afoot but Jess figured maybe surprise addled her ability to speak.

It was only when she snagged Jess's arm to keep her back that something more serious dawned.

'Gabe — you have to go and see the manager. There's been a phone call — bad news from Texas. Jess, I'll let Gabe tell you when he's spoken to Broken Bridle. All hell's broken loose at home. He has to go back. Urgently.'

Jess tried to still her pounding heart as she watched Gabe rush back down the corridor at full speed.

'What's happened?'

Nancy shook her head and tried to quash her overwhelming desire to sob. 'It's not good. Oh, Jess, it's not good at all.'

'What?'

'A fire,' she whispered.

And as Nancy burst into tears, Jess's heart slowly began to bleed for what she knew was coming.

Everything had blown apart. Now she really did have to let Gabe Garrett go.

★   ★   ★

When Gabe returned he confirmed there had been a devastating blaze in outbuildings at Broken Bridle. One that had devoured buildings like a blood-thirsty dragon, threatened lives and refused to be doused or controlled.

It was clear he'd have to leave for Texas as soon as he could.

He looked drawn and ravaged him-self.

'We've lost buildings, livestock. A

ranch hand is in a serious condition. One family has lost their home. They're devastated. I must go there.'

Jess felt herself go into shock. Although she didn't know these people personally, the looks on Nancy and Gabe's faces spoke volumes.

Now wasn't a time to take Gabe aside and shout at him — or even ask questions about his secret investment. That could wait for the future.

'Not much I can do from here. Even less on a plane — but I've said I'll head back.' He ran his hand through ruffled up hair.

Despite the shock news of the night Jess still itched to soothe him and try to take away the pain etched on his features. She knew nothing would work on that. No tincture or herbal cure could mend this disaster. Her heart went out to him.

'I can call the airline while you get yourself ready?' she offered, pushing her selfish urges aside. 'I can make arrangements with a cab firm to take you there. Leave the hire car's return to me.'

He nodded. 'Always organised and capable. I'm afraid I'm not thinking too straight,' Gabe admitted. His green eyes looked dark and his frame looked hunched by the devastating news.

'You'd have done as much for me. And neither would I be if the same thing had just happened to my business. You're still in shock.'

★ ★ ★

A few hours later he was ready to go. Jess had found him an early morning flight that would gradually and slowly connect to his end destination.

They kissed quickly and softly; one that did not impart the aching need and longing she felt inside. They were outside the hotel in the darkness and this time he didn't ask first. It was just taken as a given — they were close friends now. This was a crisis. They were still connected by a common bond

270

and compassion took over from old scores or crossed wires.

'You could come visit? I could come back here again when things calm?' Gabe assured her softly.

She pulled him close. The clothed muscle beneath her fingers stole her breath away.

'You could. Just let me know and you'll have a place to stay.'

'You'll have me back? That's progress.' He faked a grin but it had latent transparency marred by events of the day.

'Do you want me to come to the airport with you?' she offered at last in a gasped rush.

Gabe shook his head. 'If you come I may not go . . . and I have to.' His eyes grew sombre as the cab driver restarted the engine in a subtle hint. 'Look after my brother.'

Jess tried to keep the tears back. Usually she schooled herself to keep them padlocked tight. The glimmer of a tear slipped out as she closed the door and he let down the electric window to take her hand a final time.

'Take good care now.'

A few seconds later he was gone. A cowboy to commit to memory and one with hard tasks ahead of him.

He might be a surprise billionaire tycoon, but right now he was a man in a crisis.

12

Jess stared dubiously at the Lucky Star saloon bar. She was feeling not so much a fish out of water, as a fish newly landed on the moon.

Two weeks ago she'd never had considered a trip to Texas, but that was before Gabe's surprise tickets and his letter of invitation.

'I'm not sure this is such a good idea, Nancy. I'm a little travel jaded for socialising.'

'Couple of drinks, some food. I'm not expecting you to drink 'til dawn or line dance with the locals.' Nancy raised her eyes to the sky. 'They serve good meals; it's not all gun fights and western warfare here.'

Jess shook her head.

'If I drink anything you'll have to

carry me to Broken Bridle because of jet lag — can you handle lugging me into your car?'

Nancy batted her concerns away.

'I'll just get some ranch boys around to tie you to a horse. You'll make it there by morning.'

Nancy Garrett grinned to show she was kidding.

'C'mon, authentic Tall Trees Creek hospitality is a non-negotiable part of the tour.'

In spite of Jess's protests, Nancy took Jess's arm and tugged her inside the bar.

Nancy's chestnut curls bounced, her figure curvy and Texas-rose petite. Jess saw several cowboys' heads turn to watch them when they entered the dim interior of The Lucky Star.

'You're on vacation; go with the flow,' Nancy encouraged, squeezing her arm.

Jess was several thousand miles from home now. As far from her Scottish, highland village and familiar roots as she could imagine. Boy did it feel strange.

For starters it was hot. Even the air was arid and dusty, but the landscape was breathtaking — rich earth hues abounded and the sky seemed to stretch forever.

'I have a duty to help you acclimatise,' Nancy endeavoured to soothe her misgivings. Either that or she was soft-soaping. 'Plus with jet lag you just have to push through. The natives won't bite — unless you want 'em to.' Nancy grinned again and indulged in melodious laughter.

Jess gave a faux scowl then sighed.

'I can sense I'm not going to win. You're as bad as your brother.'

'You bet,' Nancy continued. 'Once you smell the food you'll know I made the right choice bringing you here for dinner.'

Jess screwed up her nose and hugged her purse close. Everything about her felt out of place here — from her red striped top, the French navy jeans and white lace-up pumps. She should just have worn a sandwich-board proclaiming her tourist status to the locals.

Here chambray and muted western shirts were the worn in and effortless norm. Even Nancy sported jeans that looked so good they could have a starring role in movies.

Nervous energy bubbled inside Jess's veins. It didn't help that she wasn't remotely hungry; the airline meal had been cardboard and mush on a plastic tray, but she wasn't ready to eat yet.

Maybe by tomorrow she'd have calmed down? Perhaps after a sleep?

'You should be grateful I've brought you here instead of the dinner offer I had from Broken Bridle. Gabe invited us but I said we had alternate plans.'

The words Broken Bridle and Gabe's name set a zillion butterflies in motion behind Jess's belly-button. She didn't want to think about the crazy somersaults of electricity in her veins. Or the mere thought of seeing Gabe Garrett again.

'I can't believe my luck that he's invited me here to meet the owner of American Luxury Hotels Corporation. Having them stock Pure Pleasures' new spa line products would boost the business no end. It's an amazing coup.'

'Well, Gabe mixes in prestigious circles,' said Nancy, hiding the whole truth about events from her Scottish visitor.

Jess didn't doubt it, what with him being an influential Dallas tycoon in his own right. But she'd never expected her business backer to launch her into a major league hotel supply opportunity. If this came off perhaps she'd forgive him for keeping his investment secret in the first place.

'He also invited us to his first private viewing of his art show at Broken Bridle. It's going to be a big deal which, given how private Gabe usually is, is remarkable in itself.'

Jess nodded her agreement.

'It's a long way to come to see some paintings. But I do believe Gabe's art may just be worth it. I knew he had talent as soon as I saw his work.'

So much for relaxing, she thought. She hadn't seen him yet and already she felt wired for their first meeting. Talking about him and pre-empting that tryst wasn't helping.

Maybe he'd be altered? Maybe they wouldn't have that same spark? Maybe coming here at all had been a mistake? But Ruth and Josh were here too and they'd worked hard to persuade her to come along.

She should have declined Ruth's encouragements and stayed home. Scotland was safer — and a far cry from this land of dust and cowboy boots, cacti and cattle hands.

'Why do you always have to make me do wild things, Nancy Garrett? You push my limits. You said I'd be having lots of mellow chill time. So far we haven't stopped.'

They took two seats at the saloon's long wooden bar. There was a well scuffed dance floor, a couple of cowboys drinking and talking, and a bartender sitting on a stool wearing ultra authentic jeans.

In nearby booths a snuggled couple exchanged sweet endearments and another group of men tucked into large plates of food. They wore no Stetsons, as if paying homage to their stomachs was a no-Stetsons zone. Was that part of the cowboy code too?

Nancy turned to her visitor, hands on hips.

'Rushing around was all part of the plan. So I guess I'll be leaving now since your real date just got here.'

Jess looked up as Gabe Garrett came striding through the saloon door looking even more breathtaking than she remembered.

★　★　★

She so didn't need this. Her heart was kicking like a rodeo mule; her breath whooshing up inside her and making her feel quite giddy.

279

Her brief dalliance with a cowboy when wedding spirits were high felt light years away. He now looked even better than when she'd seen him those few short months ago — months that had turned into a mini eternity in themselves for Jess.

She'd spent her time getting perspective. The cowboy had gone back to roaming the plains, or whatever Texas cowboy ranch owners did when they weren't running multi-billion-dollar oilfields. Instead of pining she'd concentrated on business back at home.

So what if the guy walking towards her now had been on her mind constantly.

So what if he was going to be turning up and meddling with her equilibrium again, pummelling her heart into a wounded pile of longing.

She'd survive.

Why the heck had she come?

Jess stared at Nancy.

'Now I see what your brother meant about your meddlesome ways, Nancy.'

'It got you here, didn't it? He doesn't know the lengths I went to on this one. I might've said a few white lies to both of you, but needs must.'

Jess put her head in her hands. 'Don't tell me. You tricked him too! You brought me all the way to Texas to see Gabe without his knowledge?'

'He's my brother. And I love him. I think you deserve each other. And now I'm outta here,' said Nancy and she swiftly turned tail and fled.

Jess had had a bad feeling about The Lucky Star since she'd seen it. She forced herself to sit poker straight in her seat as Gabe approached, looking like a movie star cowboy with a face that made her melt with inner need.

Confusion gripped her heart with every stride.

She was going to be strong, resilient and nonchalant, wasn't she? She had to pull herself together, however much she might be trembling inside at the very sight of him.

Is it too late for me to walk out of

here and hail a cab? she thought in panic, her mind in turmoil.

Eventually, after scowling at the table, Jess looked up as Gabe came to her. He looked puzzled and confused too. But he covered it all with a wide smile and shook his head at his disbelief of the fact she was actually there in Tall Trees Creek, Texas.

'Jess — I can't believe it. I came here to meet an old friend, or so Nancy told me . . . '

'Nancy Garrett and her meddling ways are much, much worse than we ever imagined possible. It seems she's been interfering. And telling lies. She's brought me all this way for a blind date with my secret billionaire boss. When I get my hands on her — it might just be murder!'

13

Gabe Garrett couldn't believe his eyes — or his luck. He saw Jess immediately and the world grew a zillion times brighter.

She looked stunning. Her complexion dewy, her eyes bright; her gaze latching on his as soon as he came through the door. He could hardly wait to get to the table.

He might actually forgive his sister this time. She'd brought him the one woman whom he'd never got off his mind.

'Howdy. Great to see you. Don't murder Nancy yet. She means well. She's the wild, impulsive arm of the family.'

Jess stepped forward to give him a hug.

'It's good to see you, Gabe.'

He stared at Jess to drink her in. This

was the woman who'd caused such change in him and didn't even know it.

He'd refurbished and restored the ranch. He'd come to a very workable arrangement with his cousin Rex who was now owner/manager at Broken Bridle. He'd never felt better about that in all his days. His cowboy days were gone — in their place was a world of opportunity.

He'd spent the last four months of his life reneging responsibility and handing over to a man who was going to take his family's ranch to new heights and beyond.

And now he had no guilt about it. He was loosening the reins because he was owed his own dues.

Jess smiled. 'You look good, Gabe.'

'And you. Still using those Cleopatra creams — you're your own best business advert, Jess Gilmour.'

'You're heaping on the flattery and we both know it. Do you know Ruth and Josh flew out with me? Or did your sister cover that up too?'

'I expected their arrival — not yours. They've settled in already but they never mentioned you were here. You must've been Nancy's big secret. I guess you're both paying me back for what happened to you over the investment funding?'

'Are we really going to eat here?' Jess asked. 'Please say we aren't — I can't eat a thing,' said Jess.

Gabe nodded then took her hand.

'Come on. Let's go out to the ranch and I'll give you the proper tour. I'm hosting a barbecue for a few friends and family later and if I don't get back Josh will be burning down the barn again.'

Gabe might have been surprised beyond measure but having seen her again he knew this woman was special through and through.

She deserved answers and confessions.

The time had definitely come to be fair to Jess and lay things on the line.

★ ★ ★

Why was it that as soon as you wanted to go talk to someone, the opportunities shut off like a tap at the mains?

At Tall Trees, Gabe was in the midst of his family now that Josh had returned to the fold and half the neighbourhood had come along to inspect and interrogate him. It really wasn't so very different from her own hometown after all.

Gabe had decided to throw an impromptu welcome barbecue — producing food that had guests flocking back for seconds. He did it with easy grace and aptitude for catering for the swarming assorted guests under his roof.

Tall Trees Ranch was clearly a place where all were welcomed and received exemplary hospitality. He was talking to his neighbours and friends, doing the social rounds, laughing with elderly relatives with a pride that had Jess noticing and her heart skipping beats in her chest.

She'd really missed him.

Seeing him now only underlined the impact he had on her fragile heart.

He so belonged here; you couldn't paint a picture any more beautifully to show it.

The ranch was indeed something.

Gabe told her of rebuilding out-houses and barns and accommodation. What a job his team had done and the improvements could earn them plaudits. A complex of new state-of-the-industry buildings stood like some small town in its own right in the middle of rolling dusty plains and desert scenery.

And still she wanted to talk to Gabe but no opportunity came.

Did he hate that she'd come? She couldn't rightly be sure as they'd had no time to talk.

Perhaps her confession about Nancy's blind date plan had embarrassed him and this had been his easiest route out of confessing that he really had no interest in her.

Worries and doubts clamoured in her

brain so in the end Jess straightened her spine, grabbed a wine-glass and socialised.

She was glad she did, finding out more and more about Gabe from assorted old friends, aunts and cousins and hearing stories that made her look over and occasionally catch his eye. She heard about the bursaries he backed locally. The local clinic he'd funded. The school and college scholarships and the care home he'd built.

He looked at her with a wary gaze, clearly guessing what she was up to. He even once came up and accused her of gathering evidence against him.

Maybe? Maybe she was just gathering mementos about a man she'd only realised she'd started to fall in love with. The feeling had never abated; even with distance, even with time.

'Mr. Garrett, Guru of the Barbecue, I would really like to talk to you,' she said eventually, taking the courage to slip a hand around the top of his arm to stop him in his tracks.

'Can't you stop being social host extraordinaire for one moment and just give me five minutes of your time? I'll try to keep it brief.'

'Wow. Is this revenge for how I treated you in Scotland?'

'Well. I figure you're doing now what I did then. Time for a breather? Everybody needs to rest up a little sometimes. Don't want you falling into my arms?'

'You're sure?' he said to make her laugh.

'Please. I just want to talk to you now that I'm here.'

'Anytime. Let's go visit my studio.'

He smiled warmly, laid down his can of soda and pointed in the direction of a field far from the noise and clamour of the barbecue.

★ ★ ★

The studio took Jess's breath away. It was large and airy, with amazing views and so much light, bright space to paint in. One side was completely made of glass and all around the walls were paintings — the desert, the ranch, the Texas countryside, cattle grazing, a sagebrush and tumbleweed scene with a lone cowboy on a horse.

He'd set up his own little artist's paradise here and was decorating it with incredible works of his unique, startling art.

'Have they told you their news?' asked Gabe.

Jess shook her head. 'Who?'

Gabe paused. 'Ruth. And Josh of course. She's pregnant. Expecting early next year. Isn't it wonderful?'

Tears inexplicably filled up Jess's eyes. They were tears of joy. She was amazed that her friend hadn't told her but she was very glad for Gabe that her friend had had the foresight to wait and let family be the first to know. She knew Gabe would have really appreciated that gesture.

She wiped her eyes swiftly and smiled

through the tears. Gabe put a comforting hand on her arm.

It made Jess emotional because it felt like Ruth had pulled off her own final vindication. She'd already won Gabe over, sure, but now she'd really shown him what a true lady she was. It was like coming full circle.

'She hasn't told me yet. But I'm sure she will. And I'm very glad she told you first,' Jess confided.

'So at some point I may be coming back to Scotland for a baptism. Unless they decide to bring the baby here to Texas.' Gabe walked over to the large windows that overlooked vast pastureland and Jess joined him there.

'Don't you think maybe Scotland is their home now?' Jess asked softly.

Gabe took his time then nodded. 'Yeah. Guess you're right. Scotland would be much more fitting. It's their future.'

'And talking of futures,' said Jess, 'I've been hearing about your bright artistic career. A place to study in Paris.

A show planned. Work being bought up.'

'You've been listening to the natives. Don't believe the hype. They laud me as the big hero — but I'm just an art student at the moment. And GoldWells Inc is a family affair. All of us take our share of the decisions and the glory isn't just mine.'

'They respect you as the head of the family — and they're right to. Don't play down your own merits. Or these paintings.' Jess cast out her arm to the paintings and blew out a low whistle. 'Now I know I'm talking to a talent of the future.'

'I never did find out what happened to Ben Logan,' Gabe said softly, changing the subject.

Inwardly Jess wished he hadn't. It was frustrating not to get to the nub of her feelings. She'd come all this way. They were here together; alone at last. The last thing she wanted to do was talk about a man who'd tried to trick her; attempted to do her and her business harm.

'He got a police warning. It turns out he'd been defrauding money at work. He's packed up and gone. We've a new locum doctor at the practice — she's lovely. In fact she's been dating Ray from the pub. Seems serious.'

Gabe nodded. 'Thing is, I knew I acted like a grizzly bear with a cactus-wound around Ben Logan. That was partly my fault — never trusted doctors you see. Call it a prejudice — an old hang-up. Always kinda felt that mom didn't get the medical care and attention she needed. I kept telling them she was fading fast but it made no difference. Gave me a grudge — had Mom had sons with billions in the bank then, I'd have got her better attention. I guess I sensed Ben's shady side and it reared up my inner grudges.'

'Your mother's death was nothing you need to feel guilty about,' said Jess emphatically. 'Look around at all the people at that party over there who love and respect you. Believe it.'

Gabe led her to the rear of the studio. There were several large canvases there.

'Now — let's talk about Gabe Garrett — art genius of the century!' he said in a dramatic, mocking tone. 'He's very highly sought after and he has some paintings in his vaults he'd like to share. Like this one. In fact you need to see it because it's actually yours. You'll be taking it home with you.'

Jess gasped at the picture. It showed Loch Dinnoch through the trees at sunset. And there stood a woman — watching the lapping water, as she'd been that night Gabe found her there.

'It's called Lady Of The Loch. I've actually had offers to buy it. I refused. I figured the model should get first claim. Strong ethics all the way.'

'Cowboy's code,' said Jess and smiled at him but the smile died in his eyes.

Somehow their dynamic had changed.

She felt like he was apologising — bidding her a farewell. Concluding what had been between them in the past. It was slowly smashing her heart apart to recognise it.

Jess reached out and touched his cheek. 'Gabe.'

'Don't. I miss you more than is healthy. I've thought about you every day since I left. But I'm here in Texas — with all these people who need me. They expect me to be the big benefactor with Dallas links and weighty connections. I can't go off to Scotland and let them down. I came back here, hoping I could, and I've only realised they need me more than I thought. Just like you have ties to your business. I'd love to pursue a relationship, but I still have obligations — even without a ranch to run.'

Jess came closer, trying to choose just the right words; trying to be as clear and fair as she possibly could. God knows he tempted her and attracted her. Somehow inside she felt like she was dying.

Their relationship was a vulnerable sapling that would never grow strong, firm roots. Their relationship simply had nowhere to grow. Nancy had brought her here on high hopes and misguided assumptions but Gabe was no freer than he'd ever been. She'd be selfish to expect him to change his life.

He was even more tied to his obligations than she was.

'It's for the best. Sometimes parting is the only way. I'm sorry I came all this way — but I'm glad too because we can end things like friends, can't we?' Her eyes sought out his.

'Thing is, sweetheart, I'm not sure I can do friends and slow around you. And cool is outta the question.' His jaw flexed and she could see pain in his eyes; real, raw pain. 'I can't help that. I want you so bad it's killing me. I want more than I can have or you're ready to give and I don't think it's fair on either of us to prolong or test it further. Nancy means well but she did get it wrong. We have to accept things.'

Jess felt disappointment echo like a deep, dark stone well inside her. If only they'd met under different circumstances.

'You're a good man, Gabe Garrett. A man of honour. I'm lucky to know you. Shall we go back to the party? Let's not talk any more about it.'

He took her hand from his cheek and pushed it down. 'It's OK. I'm a cowboy; we're born survivors. Loners, strong and hard. Please take the painting; it's yours and I'd like you to have it.' He sighed and then faked a bright and breezy air she knew was hollow. 'Josh promised to sing a Scottish song later and I really don't want to miss getting that on video. I can blackmail him later and let their kids watch it for comic revenge.'

Gabe took down the painting and handed it to Jess, then he walked to the door.

Jess knew she may have just arrived in Texas — but she'd soon be making plans to shorten her stay. There was no point in prolonging the agony for either of them.

14

Jess stared at the bags before her. She hadn't brought much but they felt heavy and awkward. Like it had felt saying goodbye to Gabe. In the end they'd made it brief. A peck on the cheek and muttered 'goodbyes and don't forget you're always welcomes'.

Her bags, now she watched them, were particularly cumbersome for the return journey. Maybe it was the Stetson she'd promised to bring home for Ray at the pub; a travelling souvenir junkie and past back-packer, he'd said he wanted one and Jess had wanted to indulge him. After all, he'd turned the pub around and made it his own, finally releasing her from the baggage from her past. The Crofter's Inn was Dan's baby and she'd been glad to finally say goodbye.

It would take around thirty minutes

to get through check-in at Dallas airport. She'd fly to New York and then on to Gatwick and finally a domestic flight home to Inverness. It promised a long road to home.

To think Gabe must've travelled this long when he'd wound up in her store catching her falling from a ladder. With the journey still ahead of her, she felt for him now. She wished she could just press a speed switch and get back to Pure Pleasures in a blink.

It wasn't until the stewardess on the desk was putting her through the system that her mind began to wander. And wonder.

A tourism DVD was playing on a large plasma screen beside them — images of cowboys riding plains, cowboys doing rodeo. The inimitable sprawling charm of Texas and its various highlights was there in glorious high definition.

Before she knew it Jess was watching the montage, recognising that there was indeed something strong, solid and worthy about cowboys. She was thinking of the real one she knew who was so very different to the hype — and yet so much better, too.

Gabe Garrett was an oil tycoon but ranching was in his blood. And painting was his talent. He had a lot to recommend him.

With a gulp and a count to ten, Jess summoned focus. She could feel her hands beginning to sweat as her mind began to argue with the barricaded arguments she'd stacked up to outweigh everything Gabe had said.

You love him and yet you're leaving. Why?

He's not like Dan. They're complete worlds apart. He puts you first.

It's not about time and slow and steady.

It's depth of feeling that counts.

Past snatches of conversations assaulted her — Gabe's words mostly. They lodged in her mind and if she could've shifted them by shaking her head she would've. As it was the stewardess was staring at her, asking her repeated questions she wasn't answering.

'Sorry. I'm a little disoriented today,' she said in explanation and tried super hard to focus. Soon she had her boarding pass and was ready to go.

She got through check-in, glad to be rid of her bag, but unable to rid herself of the side-effects. The doubts, the sweaty hands. The clammy feeling like she'd just made the biggest mistake of her life and every single step she took away from Tall Trees Creek was irreparable, unmitigated damage inflicted on her sanity and her future.

Was she crazy?

Eventually finding a seat in departures she used her cell phone to call Ruth.

'It's me. I know you'll think I'm crazy but now I'm about to go I can't help thinking I'm in love with Gabe Garrett and I've been lying to myself about it. And before you say I told you so, I always was a slow learner. It's just taken a while to finally sink in.'

Ruth paused down the line. 'You're OK?' Ruth quizzed.

'I'm fine.'

'I love him. But I still have to leave. My present and my future are in Scotland. Gabe's got a bright new future as an artist of repute. I can't go and wreck his dreams, make rash demands.'

'It's not flying nerves talking?'

'No. I don't mind flying. It's letting go of my personal life reins that scares me rigid. Dan made me think I was unlovable. And so gullible it hurt.'

'Sweetie, Dan really didn't deserve you.'

'Gabe said that,' said Jess.

'See, he is a good man. It's been shining bright for a while now. I'm glad you've finally seen the light.'

'But it's too late. I still have to leave,' Jess said firmly. She wouldn't, couldn't, alter her plans. Gabe was the kind of man who would give up his dreams for her — and she'd been on the losing end of a relationship like that before. 'I have to go back. I have ideas, big meetings planned.'

'Even if it means losing the love of your life?'

'I still need time to think,' said Jess.

'But you still love him, don't you?'

It was true. Clarity had dawned — so fast and thick it was like an avalanche of afterthought. Here was a man professing his love and willingness to risk his present and future on his feelings for her and she'd turned away, intent on sensible caution.

Was she a fool?

After all he'd been through himself Gabe was still open to risk his heart again for her.

In contrast Dan had been the 'rodeo showman'. The guy who'd wanted the adulation and the plaudits — the rhinestone ego boost. But he hadn't been able to choose between two women, let alone two separate worlds of deception he'd created. Instead, he'd opted for both.

Gabe was so different it stared her in

the face like a zebra crossing with neon highlights. Was she wrecking a chance of happiness with her reserve?

He wasn't asking for forever. He was inviting her to take a chance on his love.

'So you're still going home?'

'Sometimes thought is the best cure for madness,' she replied sadly.

The trouble was, Jess knew, she was petrified and she wanted Gabe so badly it made her scared to make any move. She'd sealed over her deepest longings, her love and respect, and all because Dan had let her down. She'd long suspected her dead husband's infidelity; often wondered at his frequent trips away. Later she blamed herself for hiding from it and living with the doubts.

Jess stared at the departures board.

'He's already gone to see you. He left half an hour ago,' said Ruth softly. 'It seems to me you're both slow learners — but right now you're showing some promise that you'll learn fast in the right direction.'

Jess felt her heart triple salco in her chest leaving her giddy and disoriented as if she truly were on ice skates.

'But I've gone through check-in. It's too late.'

'Go to him. To heck with check-in and plane tickets. Garrett Inc will pay your travel costs.'

Jess cleared her throat.

'I feel like if I don't go and see him now my life will never be as bright and wonderful and promise-filled again. Maybe I need to put my business second for once. I'm going back to see if he'll give me another chance.'

Ruth whooped so hard down the line Jess had to remove the phone from her ear.

'At last — eureka, she's got it!' said Ruth then blew out a long sigh. 'Should I get the airline to make a public announcement?'

'No time, I have to go find Gabe. Forget about my bag. I'll survive on hand luggage — and seize the day!'

'Go do it, babe!' Ruth urged. 'What the heck do you think we've all been pushing you towards?'

'That boring, huh?'

'Listen sweetie, this is hardly boring. Leaving it to half an hour before a flight departs to break the news to yourself that you're in love and have found the man you want to spend your future with? This is so wonderful I'm crying!'

They finished the call.

She still had no idea where her future would take her — Texas, Scotland? She just knew she had to give things a try.

Jess raced out of the departure lounge — towards her destiny — to try and find the man she loved.

'I've never been luckier since I met him,' said Jess to herself. Smiling, she ran as fast as she could towards the exit.

★ ★ ★

As Jess was hurrying out, Gabe was hurrying in, intent on making rash demands at the check-in desk and being forceful and out of character about finding the woman he loved in their departure lounge. He was intent on using the rather large Tiffany engagement ring in his pocket too.

'Miss Jessica,' he said on a breathy sigh when he ran right into her and steadied her shoulders with strong, warm hands. 'Thought I'd made a very grave mistake.'

'You're not the only one, Gabe Garrett.'

They stared for some moments as reality fought with disbelief inside them. Gabe caught her arm and gently but firmly pulled her to him, as Jess looked in complete surprise and shocked delight at the man she loved.

'I thought I'd lost you,' he said on a desperate breath. 'Thought I'd lost my chance.'

'No. For once I'm exactly where I should be,' she answered.

The man she loved heart and soul watched her with deep green, amazing eyes. A man who'd had her craving his contact, his smile, his touch. A man so in her system he already felt part of her. They had their whole lives to take things from here.

'Just glad we've both had a meeting of minds, sweetheart. Shall we go back to the ranch and think things over?' he asked in a drawl and removed his dusty, dented hat.

'I don't need to think. I just know I need to be with you. Cowboy, billionaire. Guy who paints and travels the globe finding sunsets to make spectacular . . . I'll take whatever you choose.'

She hesitated to throw him a smile.

'I found my heart in Tall Trees, Texas. It had been missing for quite a while — but now it's functioning quite well. I think it has potential after all.'

'Sure about that?' His eyes glittered. 'What about Business Woman of the Year?'

'Even business brains need sabbaticals.' She grinned. 'Never been more certain of anything. There's an ex-tyrant ranch owner that my heart's taken a shine to,' she teased.

He grinned. 'Then I've a hankering to take a detour to a quaint little place in Scotland if you'll have me. Intend to do a lotta painting there when I settle. I just have to ask the woman I love if I can stay with her first.'

'I think I can find a vacancy.'

He pulled her into his arms.

'I'm never going to do what Dan did. Swans mate for life — the Garrett men abide by the cowboy's code. You know this is no fling, no crazed un-planned flight of fancy?'

She smiled heart and soul at the man she truly loved. 'Just takes me a while to wake up and smell the coffee.'

They kissed. Inhibitions stampeded to the four winds, nothing but love and whole-hearted acceptance in their place.

'I love you, Jess Gilmour.'

'I love you, Gabe Garrett. Don't care where we live. As long as I'm with you. How do you feel about your painting?

Won't this delay things?'

'Don't give a hoot, honey. Long as it's with you. Though somewhere hot involving a bikini or two might rank first priority. Especially when we have our honeymoon. Think you'll mind if I build a stable block out back of Rowan Croft? Not planning on ranching but I've never lived without a horse.'

Jess let her head fall against his chin.

'Will you say yes if I ask you?' he said softly. 'What about considerin' me for a husband — to have and to hold?'

With a modest flourish he produced the ring box and made Jess gasp.

'I'd be honoured if you said yes. Marry me, Miss Jessica Gilmour, since you've captured my heart?'

'Most definitely. Yes. I will.'

And she kissed him from the heart.

★   ★   ★

There was huge applause in the Crofter's Flask at an exceptional performance. Nancy had just sung and wowed the crowd. She took a bow and left the stage with a sassy twirl.

These days Ray was giving her regular bookings as a singer. She combined her singing hobby with working full-time as Jess's new Pure Pleasures development manager. She was such a keen, enthused asset to the team she could've been born to it.

Jess looked around the pub she'd once owned and resented and now had passed on to a better man. All around her, their friends had gathered for a no-holds barred engagement party the likes of which Invergarry had never seen. The pub was full and fit to burst.

Gabe agreed that this was so much more them than a fancy party at one of Texas's finest hotels where they would feel awkward and trussed up.

Gabe had even flown them here by private jet from Texas this time. Now that he'd found the love of his life, he wasn't finding his billionaire status quite so problematic any more. He didn't feel he had to hide it. Sometimes money got you places faster. When you were happy and running international business affairs, you sometimes had to travel in style.

'Happy to be home — happy to be back in Scotland?' Gabe asked, holding out a hand to lead Jess out to the dance floor. She was wearing a dress the same luscious colour as her bridesmaid's dress. Gabe had later confided he'd realised he'd completely fallen in love with her that day at the wedding — when he'd seen her in that dress. He'd never forgotten the sundress she'd worn once either.

Jess grinned. She'd never been happier in her whole life.

Loving Gabe Garrett was so much better than business awards or even seeing her company thrive, grow and get praise in the lauded Beauty Bible no less.

'Enjoying your highland vacation so far, ranch boy?' Jess asked him, her tone teasing.

His hands rested possessively on her

waist and caused shivers to dance up and down her spine.

'Nowhere better, ma'am.'

'And to think I once heard a story about a Texan tourist who came here and hated the site of the place. Resented even coming,' she teased.

'This cowboy is fixin' to stay,' Gabe replied and gently kissed the woman he loved. 'Hope you rode the other guy outta town. Musta been some kinda fool to ignore the charms before him.'

Jess smiled at her fiancé.

'I hear he's a reformed character these days. In fact, he's the only man in the world for me,' she answered.

THE END